The Hesitant Heart

Also by Jane Edwards
in Large Print:

Dangerous Odyssey
Yellow Ribbons

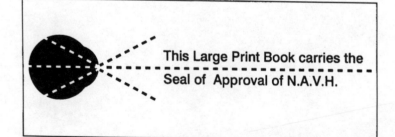

This Large Print Book carries the
Seal of Approval of N.A.V.H.

The Hesitant Heart

Jane Edwards

Thorndike Press • Thorndike, Maine

Published in 1997 by arrangement with Jane Edwards.

Thorndike Large Print ® Candlelight Series.

The tree indicium is a trademark of Thorndike Press.

The text of this Large Print edition is unabridged.
Other aspects of the book may vary from the original edition.

Set in 16 pt. Plantin.

Printed in the United States on permanent paper.

Library of Congress Cataloging in Publication Data

Edwards, Jane (Jane Campbell), 1932–
    The hesitant heart / Jane Edwards.
        p.   cm.
     ISBN 0-7862-1189-X (lg. print : hc : alk. paper)
     1. Large type books. I. Title.
  [PS3555.D933H47   1997]
  813′.54—dc21   97-21450

For Rick and Grace,
Miguel and Katherine
and Ryan Alexander

And a special note of thanks to that assembly-line crew back in Detroit who put together the Pontiac GTA Trans-Ams. "Ammie," the car in Chapter Five of this book, is real. She's mine. I love her!

Chapter One

"Sitting Tight!"

Leigh Sinclair answered the office phone in her usual, crisp way. Automatically, she began scouring her mind for available personnel. With each new service she added, her small, specialized company grew more popular. More and more, Santa Fe seemed to be clamoring for the unique protection her firm could offer.

Well, there was still Roger, Leigh realized in resignation. Roger was it, the only employee she had left to assign. Bookings for the summer were already so heavy that accepting more than one additional client would be out of the question.

"Hello?" The voice sounded somewhat distressed. "Are you the house-sitting service?"

"That's correct," Leigh said.

"Oh, thank heaven! My name is Brenda Tucker," the woman continued on a note of urgency. "I'm secretary to a rather important man here in Santa Fe. An emergency has just arisen which makes it impossible for me to keep an eye on his house while he's out of town these next few weeks. I've heard — Well, it must be an exaggeration, of course. No one could possibly furnish all the different services somebody told me were included in your contract. But if even half of what they say is true. . . ."

Leigh was used to such skeptical reaction from first-time prospects. Rather than taking offense, she laughed and said:

"I'm not sure what you've heard. It could be your informant did stretch the truth somewhat. However, Sitting Tight does provide most forms of assistance a home owner might require during his or her absence. Our company can furnish a qualified veterinarian for your employer's pets, a spraying service to keep the bugs at bay, and a professional nurseryman to doctor sick houseplants. Plumbers, electricians, a tree surgeon, and a roofer are also on twenty-four-hour call."

"You really do cope with emergencies, don't you?"

"Of course," Leigh replied matter-of-factly. "And, naturally, we install our own exclusive security system. Martindale's Sentry offers total protection for the client's property during the entire term of our contract. You need have absolutely no worry about burglars or vandals."

8

"That explains your charges, then." Already the woman's voice had grown calmer. "The expense is considerable, but it's beginning to sound as if you're worth every penny. Besides, Mr. Wainwright never minds paying for value received. Would the house-sitter occupy the premises fulltime?"

"Absolutely. For the most part, Sitting Tight's employees are college instructors or graduate students. They're available for a total commitment during the summer months," Leigh explained. "Along with the fact that everyone is fully bonded, our own comprehensive insurance takes effect the instant the security system is installed. Would you like me to furnish you with local references to reassure your employer?"

"Unfortunately he left three days ago for the Yucatán Peninsula. That's one of the things that makes this situation so difficult. But I can't wait until he can be consulted and give his okay. This morning I received a call saying that my mother, who lives in Chicago, had a bad fall and broke her hip. Mother is seventy-nine. I *have* to go and be with her."

"Of course you do," Leigh said reassuringly. The Yucatán Peninsula was about as far south as North America extended, she reflected. It was jungle territory between Mexico and the several small nations that made up Central America. Trying to contact someone down there could be terribly difficult.

"How long does your Mr. Wainwright plan to be out of town?"

"That's hard to say. It depends on how the job goes. His office is in his home. He comes and goes when it suits him. As a petrogeologist, his search for oil takes him to all sorts of out-of-the-way places. This time, I don't know if he'll be coming straight back home or stopping off for a visit with his sister in Texas."

Leigh heard the rustle of calendar pages. A dropped pen clattered across a desktop. Brenda Tucker said, "Let's make the contract for four weeks, with the option to renew for an additional two should it become necessary. Now, it is a *man* who will be taking on this job, isn't it?"

"In this instance, yes. My employee's name is Roger MacKenzie." A frown creased Leigh's forehead. "Is there any reason why it should matter?"

"Only one — a hundred-pound monstrosity of a dog named Tumbleweed, who simply cannot abide women," Brenda said. "He's a nice animal, the boss tells me — just totally

10

chauvinistic. How soon can Mr. MacKenzie start?"

"It's almost noon now. Say, three o'clock?" Leigh reached for a notepad. "Give me your address, please. Within the hour I'll dispatch a messenger with copies of the contract for your signature. As soon as that's out of the way, Kit Martindale, who handles our security arrangements, will collect the house keys from you so that he can begin installing the alarms. By mid-afternoon Roger will call on you to receive any specific instructions you wish to give about caring for the property. Okay?"

"You're a lifesaver!" After furnishing the required information, Brenda chattered on about her own plans: "There's still space on the five-forty-five flight from Albuquerque to O'Hare. With luck I can be with Mother before the hospital's visiting hours are over for the night. Thanks!"

Leigh smiled as she hung up. She found it highly satisfying, being able to assist people with their important problems and to earn an excellent living at the same time.

After notifying both Roger and the messenger service of her requirements, she dialed yet another number. The voice that answered was endearingly familiar. "Hi, Kit," Leigh greeted her former fiancé. "I hope you

11

can manage to work in a rush job for me."

An indulgent chuckle rumbled along the line. "Tell me which of your jobs isn't rush!"

"You're right, I guess. But this time we have only a few hours to put Sentry into effect. Can you cope?"

"I couldn't — for anyone except you. Do you know that in the last six months I've had to hire two extra technicians just to handle the jobs Sitting Tight sends my way? You've upgraded that part-time college job of yours into a blue-chip concern," Kit marveled. "Is everything else in your life okay, sweetheart?"

"Busy, but no complaints. How's Gail?"

"Ah, she's such a trooper." A deep love was evident in every syllable of Kit's reply. "She's having trouble getting through doors at the moment, and this July heat is draining her energy, but nary a gripe out of my lovely wife. Did I tell you the doctor says it's to be twins for sure, and possibly triplets?"

"Wow!" Leigh knew that Gail was a borderline diabetic, and that her diet and schedule required careful monitoring at all times. Especially now, during her first pregnancy, life wasn't as easy for her as for some people. But Gail refused to let anything keep her down for long. She was determined to lead a normal life in spite of her health problems.

Setting her worries aside, Leigh turned the conversation back to the job at hand. She passed along to Kit the specifics about the Wainwright property that Brenda had supplied: square footage of the house, number of entrances, distance from town, and so on. "Roger will be doing the sitting," she added. "Hopefully, this job will give him the time he needs to get all his footnotes in order for the final draft of his Ph.D. dissertation. By the way, there's a dog named Tumbleweed somewhere on the premises. He may or may not be friendly. Tell your men to watch their step."

"Will do," he promised cheerfully. "Talk to you later."

Within hours, Leigh was notified that the new job was under control. The state-of-the-art security system developed by Kit Martindale had been installed and linked to a radar-like police-surveillance scanner. Any intruder attempting to set foot on the property would be spotted as soon as he crossed a defined perimeter. Police and house-sitter would be instantly alerted. If the would-be burglar made the mistake of touching a door or window without having the proper entry code, he would be put out of commission.

Insurance coverage had also been activated. And, bearing his books and boxes of study materials, all pertaining to New Mexico's early history, Roger MacKenzie had moved into the Wainwright house. He reported back to Leigh that evening:

"The dog isn't bad. Actually, I think he's a junkfood addict with a sweet tooth. He ate my last slice of pizza and two candy bars that I hadn't even taken out of their wrappers."

"What's the house like?"

"Nice. Large. A janitorial service comes by twice a week to keep the place looking totally unlived in." Roger's idea of a lived-in look included stacks of clutter piled on every available surface. "But I think you'd like it, Leigh. The rooms are big and airy, and there's a great view of the mountains." He sighed. "I suppose I'll be better off here this summer than I would have been out wandering around in the desert."

"But you aren't positive? Historians!"

Leigh had known Roger for a number of years. Most of the time he was totally immersed in his research. He showed very little incentive to complete his studies, pick up his advanced degree, and move on to some gainful occupation. Privately, she considered him the perfect example of a career student.

In her spare time the previous winter, Leigh had helped Roger organize the study materials for his investigation into the fabled

14

Seven Cities of Cibola. With a group from the university, he had planned an extensive field trip for the months of May and June. It was a crushing disappointment to him when, at the last minute, his colleagues bowed out of the undertaking, which had been to retrace the expedition led by Francisco Vásquez de Coronado in 1540 in search of the legendary settlements.

Disappointment or not, Leigh could scarcely believe Roger's nerve when he called her only four days after having accepted the assignment at the Wainwright home. Highhandedly, he requested that she provide an immediate replacement for him.

"Leigh, it's a miracle! You'd never dream what I've found buried in this mountain of research material I brought out here with me!" Excitement tripped up his tongue. He sounded intoxicated with the prospect of success. "Proof! Proof positive that Coronado was hoodwinked into believing that the Seven Cities were only poor Zuni villages."

"That's nice, Roger. Could you tell me all about it tomorrow? It's after five already. I'm about to melt from the heat, and I was on my way —"

"Me too," he interrupted. "Want to be on my way, that is. I figure it'll take me the rest

15

of the night to map out my route. . . ."

A feeling of impending doom rolled over Leigh. It had been a long day, beset with tax problems and a broken air conditioner. She'd been looking forward to a cool, refreshing swim and then an evening curled up with a book, a nice, modern-day romance having absolutely nothing to do with either small-business accounting or probing into some mouldy old legend.

"Nothing doing, Roger. You signed a contract."

"The pointer I ran across should lead me straight to the treasure troves," he wheedled. "It will be the most monumental discovery since Howard Carter and his Egyptologists stumbled across King Tut's tomb in 1922!"

"Yes, and the most monumental curse heaped on anybody's head since then too," she replied threateningly. "Now look, Roger. You know you were the only house-sitter I had available for that job. I need you right here in Santa Fe!"

"Oh, you'll find a solution, Leigh. You always do," Roger declared in his best ivory-tower manner. "Why not take over for me yourself? There's a gorgeous pool out here, with a diving board, and surrounded by a lovely garden. Plenty of privacy, yet an easy

16

drive to work. Much more comfortable than town this time of year. I'll start packing."

"Don't you dare!" Leigh's tone was furious. "Darn you, Roger MacKenzie! I have a business to run, and our customers expect someone on the premises full-time. You contracted to take on this job. You're going to stay right there either till it's finished or till I can find someone totally reliable to take over!"

"All Seven Cities, Leigh! I'll be world famous. And when they write my name in the history books, I'll tell them that you helped."

But she proceeded to hang up. This wasn't the first time such a problem had arisen. Granted, most of the graduate students who worked for her were slightly more practical than Roger. Every so often, though, a piece of engrossing research would beckon, or the opportunity would arise to track down a shard of pottery thousands of years old. Then off they would go, leaving her holding the bag. Or, in this case, the house.

"I just hope you appreciate what I'm sacrificing for you," she snapped at Roger the next morning. She carried her suitcase into the foyer of the house, then returned to her car for the telephone answering machine and the thick blue ledgers that were essential in

17

keeping her business up to date. She noticed without surprise that Roger was completely packed, down to the last paper clip. "Okay," she said, "where's this vicious brute of a dog who eats candy bars, wrapper and all?"

"Vicious? Tumbleweed? Don't be silly." Roger snickered. "I consider him to be the dieting man's best friend."

Leigh eyed his incipient paunch. "Unlike some people, I don't need to diet. It will serve you right if the desert sweats you right down to skin and brain."

For her first meeting with the reputedly female-hating mongrel, Leigh had dressed in well-worn jeans and a loose, long-sleeved cotton shirt. Since she never wore a speck of makeup, that was no clue to her sex. Her hair, with its riotous light brown ringlets, was as short as that of many boys. Even so, as the huge, sand-colored beast came loping in her direction, she earnestly wished her wardrobe had run to a suit of armor.

Tumbleweed bounded into her arms before she could prepare a defense. A moment later she was flat on her back and a busy pink tongue was giving her face the abrasive licking of its life.

"Don't get conceited. He's just looking for candy," Roger said. "Well, thanks for coming. I'll be on my way. Want me to help you up before I leave?"

"My pal!"

Two minutes later the exhaust of the historian's four-wheel-drive vehicle was vanishing in the direction of the Sangre De Cristo Mountains. Leigh sat up to find Tumbleweed's huge yellow eyes still fixed intently on her. He didn't seem to be thinking of her as a girl. More like a five-foot-tall peppermint stick.

"You and I should have a chat about calories and tooth decay," she said.

But her grin told him this was an idle threat. Though a health enthusiast herself, she suspected that this big dog would tolerate no meddling when it came to his love of sweets.

Outside, the heat of the high desert was a force to be reckoned with. But Leigh soon found that the house's thick adobe walls and its roof of rounded, red clay tiles kept it naturally cool inside. The furnishings were Spanish, dark wood elaborately carved. However, the rooms were uncrowded, and the upholstery fabrics, of pale and tranquil colors, gave an air of peaceful comfort. Adding to the cool effect was the fact that large squares of ceramic tile had been used as the flooring material. There were plenty of small, eye-catching rugs, however, and in several of the main rooms Leigh noticed massive stone fireplaces. During the winter, the house would be a cozy refuge against the cold.

One wing of the rambling home contained a number of guest bedrooms and baths. All were pleasantly furnished, ready for occupation at a moment's notice. At the end of the west wing, a well-equipped home gym adjoined the master suite.

Fitness being part of her own daily routine, she couldn't resist a walk-through of the exercise center. A glimpse of the next room caused her to detour over to the doorway of the large bed-sitting room.

Leigh felt a rush of pleasure. Here, warm colors predominated. In decorating his own quarters, the owner of the house had shown a preference for hues more vivid than those used elsewhere in the house. Tangerine, rust, lime green, and orange had been pleasingly combined with ivory and brown, and an occasional stripe of pale citrus yellow.

The decor was so joyous that Leigh felt drawn into its center. For the first time she found herself wondering what sort of person Brenda Tucker's boss might be. The variety of tones and textures exhibited in the generous use of wood, glass, and stone made her guess him to be a man who enjoyed the sensation of touch. What a delight on bare feet the sculptured handwoven rug would be. Especially if one stepped onto it from the adjoining smooth, cool tile. Her toes curled. She blushed, embarrassed to realize that she was intruding on a client's privacy by being in this room at all. The first rule of Sitting Tight was that the company's employees were specialized caretakers — period. Snooping through a client's home was definitely taboo.

Starting to back away, Leigh's eye was caught by a pair of color photographs in large, gleaming frames. Their subjects were so appealing that she was drawn forward for a closer look.

In the first portrait, a beautiful young woman with delicate features and very dark hair gazed into the adoring eyes of a slim, fairer-skinned man. The passage of time was evident in the second picture. Twenty years or so had passed. The couple exchanged glances of undiminished ardor, but now, in addition to each other, their smiles embraced three beaming children. Leigh saw a shy, pretty girl in her late teens, a dark, handsome boy of about twelve, and a small, pert child seated on her mother's lap.

A sharp jab of envy riddled Leigh's composure. To her chagrin, she felt her eyes smart, then brim. There was so much love for one another expressed in those five faces. How wonderful it would have been to be part of a family like that!

The spurt of raw emotion had taken her by surprise. Flustered, astonished that such a thing should have happened in spite of her success at coping with life on her own, Leigh turned and fled from the room without a backward look. Such behavior was absolutely inexcusable, she told herself. Hurrying away, she went in search of quarters that would keep her as far as possible from that distracting room.

She found what she sought in the opposite wing of the house, next to the kitchen. Small, plainly furnished, the room commanded a view of the lush walled garden and a corner of an inviting turquoise pool.

An hour later, after a refreshing dip, Leigh reflected that perhaps Roger hadn't done her such a disservice, after all. Not that she would ever tell *him* that. Someone who went off in July to hunt for the Seven Cities of Cibola, of all things! Next time, he might decide to map out all eight hundred rooms of the ancient Pueblo Bonito, built by the cliff-dwelling Anasazi Indians. Or he'd try to trace the designs of the intricate robes those people had fashioned centuries earlier from turkey feathers!

★ ★ ★

During the next two weeks, Leigh and Tumbleweed settled into a comfortable routine. She had no idea why Brenda Tucker had claimed that the animal didn't like women. He and she went out for a long romp every morning and evening, and got along beautifully.

Her business continued to run smoothly from its temporary headquarters. Leigh kept the bookkeeping up-to-date, scheduled advance reservations for clients requiring house-sitters during the autumn months, and considered applications from service firms eager to do business with Sitting Tight. Once a day she checked with all seventeen of her employees keeping watch over properties in and around Santa Fe. She also managed a brief daily chat with Gail.

"I seem to be looking more like Moby Dick all the time," Kit's wife confided with a laugh about two and a half weeks after Leigh had taken over from Roger. "How about you? Are you sleeping all right out there in the boondocks?"

The Wainwright home was four miles out of town. "You make it sound as if I'm stuck in a cactus halfway to Taos. Sure, I'm sleeping well."

When, hours later, she awoke, Leigh

thought at first it was a dream about that conversation that had dragged her from slumber. Within seconds, though, she realized how wrong that guess was. Gail's concern about her sleep wasn't causing the persistent buzz from the device on her nightstand. Sentry's first-stage alarm was humming urgently away in the darkness!

An intruder had invaded the grounds!

Chapter Two

The raspy drone continued, frazzling Leigh's nerves. With a shiver she reached for her robe and belted it tightly around her pink, summer-weight pajamas. Starting to switch on the bedside lamp, she stayed her hand. It would be foolish to let the intruder know his approach had been detected. Let him come ahead and take the consequences.

She reassured herself that there was no cause for worry. Help should already be on its way.

She gulped, hoping that was the case. Of all the times to start remembering Gail's comments about the isolated location of this place! Leigh had perfect faith in Kit's invention. Sentry was a unique home-security system that had been tested many times.

But maybe, she thought, it wouldn't hurt to give the police a ring, just in case their power was off or something. Best to make sure they had noticed the alarm and were responding. After all, this house and its contents were her company's responsibility.

Thanks to the bright moonlight flooding

through the sheer bedroom curtains, she was able to find her way easily about. Slippers forgotten, Leigh made for the door. There was an extension phone in the kitchen, and she could reach it in seconds. But just as she gained the hall, an ominous grating sound replaced Sentry's original warning buzz.

She flung a frightened glance back at the alarm device. Along with each of her employees, Leigh had undergone a training session to learn how Kit's unique instrumentation worked. The alarm had three distinct tones, so that the alerted householder could tell exactly how close an intruder had come. In addition, the security box was equipped with buttons that lit up to indicate where the incursion was being made.

Sure enough, one of the buttons was now glowing. As yet, it was only amber, meaning that the trespasser was still outside a fifteen-foot perimeter. But, unfortunately, he and she seemed to be headed in the same direction.

Only the thought of Tumbleweed's massive presence gave Leigh the courage to continue into the kitchen. She found the dog already on his feet. His back was rigid, his shaggy muzzle pointed straight at the double-locked back door. With jittery fingers, she reached for the telephone receiver. Suddenly, she dropped it back on its hook as the last sound in the world she would have expected to hear met her ears.

A whistle! Rather than exercising cautious stealth, this burglar had the nerve to approach the house with a jaunty whistle on his lips!

Tumbleweed's response was instantaneous. His deafening bark caused Leigh to jump and stub her toe against the base of a cupboard. That would do it, she thought, relieved in spite of her conviction that it was better to have the intruder apprehended than running around loose, menacing other people's homes. But that barking would surely send any sensible burglar in the business hightailing for Albuquerque.

Astonishingly, it did not. Unbelievable as it seemed to Leigh, not even the loudly announced presence of a watchdog succeeded in halting his advance. The scrape of metal against metal caused her to catch her breath in dismay. He had come prepared with a skeleton key!

From her room down the hall came a shrill, urgent din. Sentry was cutting loose with its final phase warning. By now, Leigh knew, the back-door button would be glowing bright red. Step by step, the mechanism was responding exactly as it had done during

27

her training session.

No longer was there any doubt in her mind as to the next development. Clenching her fists, she took a deep breath and waited.

There was time for one last rattle of the key. Then the cheeky whistle faded into a tuneless hiss and ceased abruptly. A heavy thud shuddered against the door's outer panel. Seconds later the porch shook as the burglar collapsed.

Leigh's heart was pounding like a runaway freight train. And Tumbleweed seemed upset too. He whined, his yellow eyes swinging toward her, then back at the door in mystification.

"It's okay, boy," she tried to reassure him. "He's a bad guy or he wouldn't be out there. And that'll never happen to you and me because we know how to stay friends with Sentry."

A precise code pressed into the outside monitoring device would disarm the system. But should this precaution not be taken, drastic results occurred the instant a door or window was touched.

Leigh shivered at the thought of the fate that had befallen the burglar. The moment he had inserted that skeleton key into the lock, a dose of odorless but extremely potent gas had been emitted. Though non-toxic, it was designed to quickly stun an interloper. The gas would render him unconscious for about seven minutes, allowing him to regain consciousness just in time to be taken into custody.

Like Leigh, Tumbleweed heard the wail of the approaching siren. He bounded to the door, scratching at it in agitation.

"Take it easy," she said, trying to calm her loyal friend. "There's no need to eat him. The police will be here in a minute. They'll take care of everything."

Remembering that Sentry was still primed to repel unwanted company, she ran down the hall to the foyer. There she flipped several levers on the central control panel, disengaging the potent system for the time being. She had barely finished when two patrol cars spurted into the driveway, their dome lights hurling bolts of red and blue through the clear night air. Leigh waited until the sirens ceased. Then, quickly explaining what had happened, she directed one pair of officers around to the back of the house.

The other two men accompanied her inside. Both halted at the entrance to the kitchen, startled by the sight of a hundred-pound mongrel trying to claw his way through the door.

"Get that dog under control, lady," the

officer in charge ordered tensely. "We don't want any blood spilled here."

Leigh opened a drawer, removed a seldom-used leash, and snapped it onto Tumbleweed's collar. Turning back, she saw that her companions were concentrating on the intruder. The anaesthetizing gas seemed to be wearing off. She stepped out of the way, hauling the dog with her, as the policemen hoisted the reviving man to his feet and marched him into the kitchen.

"Get your hands off me!" he cried.

Leigh caught her breath. The slim man in the leather jacket seemed highly indignant at being taken into custody. She'd have thought that a professional burglar would expect to run into that problem now and then, but he was acting as if everyone except him was in the wrong. In an earthy mixture of English and Spanish he expressed his views at being frisked for a weapon.

"There'd better be a good explanation —"

Before he could finish his sentence the agitated dog whined, and it seemed to Leigh he was preparing to launch himself forward.

"Tumbleweed, stay!" she cried.

The burglar's dark head snapped around. For the first time he caught sight of Leigh. The fury in his brown eyes increased as he took in her petite, pajama-clad figure, her

bare feet, the small hands straining at the leash.

"How did you get into the house?" he snapped at her. "And what kind of spell did you put on the dog? He *hates* women!"

"Oh, sure," Leigh responded. "Anyone can tell he's about to beat me to death with that big, wet tongue of his. Right after he finishes eating you for a midnight snack."

"Let him go and see what happens."

"Come along peacefully now," one of the officers intervened, none too anxious to have a beast the size of Tumbleweed on the loose. "There's been enough trouble."

"You haven't even *begun* to see trouble!" The man's tone was ominous. "Let go of my dog!"

The possessive pronoun took Leigh by such surprise that she dropped the leash. Tumbleweed had obviously just been staying beside her out of courtesy. Now, freed from restraint, he hurtled forward. From the instant of the impact it was quite apparent that the dog was besotted by the mysterious dark stranger.

Leigh gasped. "How 'bout that? He took to me right off too."

"I find that extremely hard to believe."

The man's gaze lingered on her, and she frowned. She felt certain she had never met this most unusual burglar anywhere before. Yet he did look oddly familiar. The few times he'd stopped scowling, she'd caught just a hint of an intriguing resemblance to someone.

Before she could grasp the elusive memory, he broke the gaze to turn back to the officers. "I believe I've proven my point, officers. *I* am not the intruder here. *She* is."

A tingle of uneasiness wiggled up Leigh's spine. Though she had lived in Santa Fe her entire life, she had never happened to meet any of these policemen in person. Already, she'd gotten a couple of hesitant looks from them. She drew herself up to her full five feet zero and proceeded to refute the accusation.

"I hope you don't intend to take his word for it," she said in a businesslike tone. "I'm Leigh Sinclair, and my firm, Sitting Tight, was hired to protect these premises during the owner's absence. If you will get in touch with Mr. Kit Martindale, who designed the security system, he will be more than happy to vouch for me."

She could tell from the immediate lessening of tension that they recognized Kit's name. So far, her rebuttal seemed to be going very well. Leigh smoothed back her short mop of curls, wishing she could muster more height and more dignity. It wasn't easy in bare feet.

Tumbleweed gave a couple of short, encouraging yelps. She avoided the four-legged traitor's gaze. Without a doubt, Leigh thought glumly, Tumbleweed had smelled jelly beans or Tootsie Rolls on the man who'd tried to force his way into the house, and he had been corrupted by his insatiable craving for sweets.

"Perhaps," she suggested, "if this person isn't a burglar, he would kindly explain what he is doing here in the middle of the night?"

Without a word, the burglar unzipped one of the pockets of his leather jacket. From it he pulled a wallet. Pieces of identification seemed to flow from the see-through holders. Exhibiting each item to her abashed gaze before presenting it to the officer in charge, he held up an American Express card, a driver's license from the State of New Mexico, something official-looking from the FAA, which shot past her nose too quickly to identify, and a stack of embossed business cards.

"I'm here," he said, "because I live here. My name is Carlos Wainwright."

An awkward silence fell over the kitchen. Leigh studied the deeply tanned face. It was possible, she thought in resignation. Though nobody had ever mentioned his first name in her hearing, this man could very well be Brenda Tucker's boss. Undoubtedly, he had seemed familiar to her earlier because of her glimpse of him in that family portrait in his bedroom. The twelve-year-old had grown up.

"Mr. Wainwright . . ." she murmured.

The beginnings of a victorious smirk tugged at the corners of his mouth. It gave her some idea of how good looking he'd be if he ever got around to smiling in earnest. She doubted that would happen anytime soon. His expression turned grim again when she courteously requested that he tell her his secretary's name and state his whereabouts for the past few weeks. Those glowering dark eyes bore right through her as he furnished the correct information.

She sighed in relief, then glanced apologetically at the policemen. "I'm sorry you were called out, officers. We seem to have a false alarm here. If you wish, I'll come down to the station tomorrow morning and fill out a report."

"Tomorrow morning, nothing! You'll accompany them down to the station this very minute," said the man whose unheralded arrival had caused all this trouble. "How do I know *you're* not a burglar?"

It took another two hours to settle matters to everyone's satisfaction. As it happened, the night sergeant knew both Leigh Sinclair and Carlos Wainwright by sight, but there were more explanations to be furnished, and release papers to sign. It was almost four in the morning by the time they walked sleepily out to the curb where Kit's van was parked.

In response to Leigh's call, the redheaded young inventor had leaped out of bed and hurried down to the station to act as her character witness. Now he gave her an affectionate hug before holding open the vehicle's door to usher her inside.

"Is everything okay now?"

"Sure. I appreciate your coming, Kit. Things always seem less burdensome when you're around." She caught sight of Carlos Wainwright, who had paused rather uncertainly on the sidewalk some distance behind them. "The police took us in together, in one of their squad cars. Would you mind running him home too, please?"

The man she had mistaken for a burglar overheard her appeal and her friend's polite but unenthusiastic assent. His shoulders stiffened. Clearly, he would have preferred to refuse. But it was chilly outside, and taxis at that time of night were few and far between.

"Thank you," he muttered, and climbed into the back of the van as soon as Kit had shifted several boxes of equipment.

Leigh wasn't much of a night owl, and she found it an effort to keep her eyes open as they wound through the quiet, narrow streets. Familiar landmarks kept her from giving in to drowsiness. She had always thought it strange that although Santa Fe was by far the oldest capital city in the United States, New Mexico had been one of the very last states to be admitted to the Union. And even loyal natives insisted that nothing had been done to widen the streets around the city center since they were first laid out around 1610.

Kit passed the venerable San Miguel Mission, then took the Canyon Road east out of town. He caught Leigh's eyes as she smothered a yawn, and grinned. "Been quite a night, I gather."

"I'll say," she agreed. "Nothing I'd want to repeat, that's for sure. But it was almost worth the fright and inconvenience to see how wonderfully Sentry worked!"

From the back of the van came a snort. Kit eyed his passenger through the rearview mirror. "As I told you before, Mr. Wainwright, I'm sorry about the mix-up. My security system was designed to protect home owners and their property, not to lay them low."

"I can vouch for its efficiency in all respects."

"But I shouldn't ask you for an endorsement, right?" Kit shrugged, then nudged Leigh as he pulled to a halt in the driveway of the large, Spanish-style home. "Get your stuff, sweetheart, and I'll drive you to your apartment. Either that or you can come on back to the house with me for what's left of the night."

"What about my car?"

"The electronics team can pick it up tomorrow morning when they deactivate Sentry."

"Okay. Thanks." Muffling another yawn, Leigh started to climb out of the van. Before her foot touched cement, Carlos Wainwright had scooted out and was extending a hand to help her down.

"Listen," he said, "I'm sorry about my attitude earlier. It was stupid to insist on having the cops pull you in; I knew you were no more a burglar than I was."

"Oh, forget it," Leigh told him. His hand was strong and warm. She disengaged her own and took a step away. Unlike many men, he wasn't so tall that she had to peer a couple of miles up into the stratosphere just to watch his expression. To a short girl like herself, that was a real plus. "In view of everything that's happened, we'll simply cancel the balance of the contract."

"No, no, that's not what I want." There was an earnest petition in his dark eyes as he moved to close the gap between them. "I'd rather you stayed. Never mind why. Just take my word that I have a good reason for asking."

Intent on each other, neither of them had noticed Kit hop out of the driver's seat. He strode around to push his way between them. "And she has a real good reason for declining. Thanks, but no thanks."

Leigh shot him an exasperated glance. There were times, she thought, when he took his role as her protector a bit too seriously. "Kit, please!"

Returning her attention to the other man, she gave her head a firm shake. "I'm sorry, Mr. Wainwright. Now that you're home again, you have no further need for a house-sitter."

"Yes, I do," he insisted, studiously ignoring Kit. "In the first place, I'm back only temporarily. As soon as I check out the trouble I've been having with my plane, I'm going to be heading right out again. I have a business trip to make, and after that there's a family matter I have to take care of. The two together will undoubtedly keep me away for a week. Maybe more."

Brenda Tucker had mentioned something about her boss making a visit to his sister in Texas on his return trip from the Yucatán, Leigh remembered. It sounded as if he did an awful lot of traveling.

Her interest piqued, she took a closer look at his leather jacket, the type often wore by fliers. "You flew home tonight?" she asked. "Yourself?"

"Sure," he answered matter-of-factly. "A few years ago I leveled off a stretch of flat, open land behind my house. To make a night landing, all I need to do is flip on a remote-control gadget to activate the runway lights. It's as easy as working a garage-door opener."

He must have walked across the fields, then. That was why he'd approached the house by way of the back door.

For the first time Leigh noticed the weary slump of his shoulders. Lines of fatigue fanned out on both sides of his tired eyes. Rested, he would undoubtedly look different. More easygoing. Younger. She realized now that he was not much older than Kit.

And that he was probably very nice deep down inside. When pushed into a corner, though, as he had been tonight, he had instinctively adopted the bearing of an *hidalgo caballero* — an aristocratic gentleman — which came so naturally to his Spanish ancestors.

She wondered how far he had flown in the past twenty-four hours, and how serious a problem with his aircraft he'd needed to battle while in flight. Enough, she guessed, to bring him very close to exhaustion. At least for what was left of the night, he represented no threat to her. As for herself, she was too exhausted to want to spend two hours packing up her clothes and office equipment while keeping poor Kit waiting.

"We can talk everything out tomorrow," she decided. "Later *today,* I mean, when everybody wakes up. All three of us are dead on our feet." She took Kit's hand. "Thanks again for being around when I needed you. I'll call you in a few hours, or whenever I can pry open my eyelids and start thinking straight again."

Kit hesitated. Her added reminder that he might very well be needed at home finally got him moving. After a last mistrustful look in the other man's direction, he climbed back into his van and drove away.

"Careful," Leigh warned as Carlos started up the walk ahead of her. "Sentry doesn't play games, remember."

Quickly, he stepped back to allow her to precede him. Leigh traced her fingers across a series of buttons on a metal plate mounted inconspicuously alongside the door. Then she pressed the palm of her hand flat against the wood, just above the polished knob. The almost inaudible whining sound ceased.

"What?" His tone was sardonic. "No need to say 'open sesame'?"

"These days, the correct entry code is sufficient."

Leigh stepped inside as Carlos flipped switches to turn on lights. He cleared his throat before she could start down the hall to her room.

"Uh, I just wanted to say thanks for sticking around tonight," he said. "It was pretty obvious your boyfriend didn't want you to stay."

"Kit?" Leigh smiled. "He's not my boyfriend. But you're right. He didn't want me to stay. I wouldn't have if we all hadn't been ready to drop. As a businesswoman in this town, maintaining a spotless reputation is vitally important to me, and I can't risk being talked about."

"I know what they'd say, and it wouldn't

be true. But just so that they never get the chance, tonight you may have Tumbleweed as your bodyguard." Carlos Wainwright's grin looked almost boyish. "And tomorrow I'll find you a real *duenna,* the sort of chaperone not even that guy out there in the van could complain about. Good night, Miss House-Sitter."

Chapter Three

It was past ten o'clock when Leigh entered the kitchen. Tumbleweed trotted contentedly at her heels. They found Carlos at the round dinette table with a plate of golden-brown waffles and luscious link sausages in front of him. The wonderful aroma of just-perked coffee filled the room.

"It smells great in here," she said, pouring herself a cup.

When Carlos pointed to a warming tray in the oven, she nodded eagerly, removed it, and joined him at the table.

"Feeling better?" he asked.

"Much." As she reached for the syrup, Leigh saw that his crisp black hair was still wet from his shower. No lines of fatigue showed on his well-scrubbed face this morning. He was dressed in khakis, ankle-high boots, and a colorful terrycloth shirt. "Looks like you've perked up too," she said.

"A few hours of sleep was all it took. Good thing," Carlos added in resignation. "Looks as if I'm due to spend most of the day poking and prodding around inside an engine."

"Your plane's?" Leigh tried to hide her surprise. He didn't look like the type of person who had ever encountered a spot of grease firsthand.

He immediately corrected this misapprehension. "I've taken several courses in aviation maintenance. Usually, I have a professional mechanic check my work over when I'm through tinkering, just as a safety precaution. But sometimes my explorations take me hundreds of miles from the nearest hangar. By knowing how to trace a break in an electrical line or to clean a clogged fuel filter, I stand a much better chance of emerging unscathed in case I'm forced down."

Leigh thoroughly approved of this practical point of view. He seemed to know how to do a lot of things, she thought as she took the last bite of her sausage. They included cooking a very tasty meal.

"I'd better show you how to manipulate Sentry's gadgetry so you can let yourself back into the house safely," she offered. "That is, if the security system and I are really going to stay. Are you sure you want us to? It costs quite a bit of money to hire Sitting Tight."

"To tell the truth, I'm hoping that by doing so, I can save a small fortune." Carlos set his dishes in the sink. "Why don't you let that gizmo baby-sit the house for now and come take a walk across the fields with me? A brisk hike would do us both good. Especially since we've slept so late and haven't the time today to do a good aerobics workout."

Leigh remembered the gym at the opposite end of the house. She couldn't help noticing the sleek, firm biceps swelling the short sleeves of his shirt. Apparently, he enjoyed staying in shape.

So did she. "I'd like to see your plane," she said. "On the way out there, you can tell me what you meant by saying my company might be able to save you some money."

Once they had set out, though, he didn't seem at all anxious to broach the subject. Leigh didn't push. His distracted expression gave her the impression that he regretted having said even as much as he had.

Adroitly, he switched topics. "How do I rate having the boss of the outfit take on my house as her personal assignment?"

"Believe me, I was your last resort." With a rueful laugh, Leigh explained how Roger MacKenzie's determination to renew his search for the Seven Cities of Cibola had left her in the lurch.

"I wouldn't want you to get the notion that my employees are unreliable," she added. "For the most part, they are serious scholars — young instructors and graduate students.

45

For them, house-sitting is a great job. It leaves them plenty of time to study and write, and pays their expenses while they're working toward their degrees." She sighed. "Once in a while, though, the field-research bug bites them. That's when I find myself out on a limb."

"Are *you* an experienced house-sitter?"

"Am I! I house-sat constantly my last two years of college, because I couldn't afford to pay the rent on an apartment."

Leigh wished she had simply said "yes" and let it go at that, because Carlos asked next, "Weren't your parents able to help?"

Talking about her past was something she avoided whenever possible. Another person would have received a short, sharp answer. But the man striding across the open countryside next to her wasn't someone to be dismissed so curtly. If she intended to go on working for him — and that was by no means decided yet — she probably owed him a courteous reply, even if her past was none of his business as a client.

"There were savings enough to cover my first two years of higher education," she said, managing to dodge the real issue. "After that, life became more of a struggle. But we managed."

"*We?*"

Leigh detoured around one of the giant Saguaro cacti dotting the arid landscape. The high desert had a fascinating life of its own. Not everyone appreciated its stark beauty, of course, or the harsh dun coloring of the countryside during the hotter months. Leigh loved it in all seasons.

"Kit and I," she replied finally, when he continued to wait for her to explain. "We managed."

That haughty, oh-so-Spanish look tightened Carlos's features. "I see."

"No, you don't. But never mind."

"I thought you said he wasn't your boyfriend."

"And he isn't. He's my former fiancé."

Her answer caught him by surprise. "Former? When he still calls you 'sweetheart'?"

"He always has."

"What do you call *him?*"

Exasperation began to seep into Leigh's voice. "I call him 'Kit,' " she said. "It's short for 'Christopher.' "

Carlos scowled. "Do you still love him?"

"Of course. I always have."

"Then why —"

Leigh lengthened her stride and forged on ahead. Sometimes she liked Carlos Wainwright and sometimes she didn't. Either way, he was too darned persistent for his own good. As far as she was concerned, that particular conversation was now ended. She had answered his questions truthfully. If that wasn't good enough for him, too bad. Had she not been so interested in seeing his plane up close, she'd have turned around and marched right back to the house.

The sleek little aircraft was a beauty. It was painted a gleaming white with stark black identification numbers preceded by an "N." Inside, there was room for a copilot on the right side of the cockpit and for six passengers in the cabin.

"Or the seats can be removed to make room for cargo," Carlos explained. "Sometimes I bring home rocks that catch my fancy."

"Oil-bearing shale?" Leigh guessed.

His dark eyes narrowed. "Where would you get an idea like that?"

"Oh, for heaven's sake!" Leigh wasn't used to dealing with such touchy people. What was he so suspicious about? "I got an idea like that from the fact that your secretary described you as a petro-geologist. That *is* someone who studies rock formations in a search for oil, isn't it? Or do I have my terms wrong?"

"No, you're quite right. I'm sorry to sound

48

so prickly," Carlos surprised her by apologizing. "It's just —"

She looked at him and waited, just as he had waited for her to explain about her relationship with Kit. The silent query worked. He swung an arm as if striking out at an enemy.

"Someone keeps jumping in and stealing my discoveries out from under my nose. I don't know who or how. It's driving me loco!"

Leigh's big blue eyes widened in understanding. "That's why you were so furious to find me in your house last night, wasn't it? It wasn't just because Sentry had zapped you. You really did suspect that I might be a thief."

"Well, I was in kind of an ugly mood after battling engine trouble for a hundred and fifty miles. Finding someone making herself at home in my house was the last straw. But I should have figured that an actual thief wouldn't be running around in her pajamas."

"Have there been break-ins in the past?"

"I don't think so. None that I've managed to detect, anyway." Carlos looked both angry and baffled. "None of my papers have disappeared. Yet, somehow, someone is finding out what's in my reports almost before I get my notes in order."

"Does your secretary enter the information into a computer? You hear a lot about hackers penetrating access codes, stealing secrets, finagling bank accounts, and even jeopardizing national security just by finding out a few key words."

"Like in *War Games*, huh?"

Both of them had seen that heart-stopping movie in which a teenage computer buff accidentally brings the world to the brink of nuclear war. It was terrifying to think that such things might actually occur. But it wasn't the right explanation for what had been happening to Carlos's discoveries.

"Brenda uses an ordinary electronic typewriter," he said. "I offered to buy a word processor for our office, but she didn't want any part of it. Besides, this last time —"

Leigh took a shot in the dark: "You didn't tell her about what you'd found?"

"I didn't tell *anyone!* But the information *still* leaked out. For the life of me, I can't see how it was possible. Six weeks ago I conducted an exploratory probe of a desert area southeast of Tucumcari. I was completely alone. There wasn't a road within forty miles of where I set down. And I'd certainly have heard another plane or copter if one had come close enough to pinpoint my location."

He gestured for Leigh to precede him

down the plane's narrow aisle. "I took nothing but penciled notes on a memo pad that never left my pocket. Yet, by the time I got home, ran a couple of chemical tests, and did a quick soil analysis, it was already too late. A claim had been staked to the mineral rights on that parcel of ground."

"Couldn't you identify your claim jumper by finding out who recorded the option?"

"It was the first thing that occurred to me. The claim was registered in the name of a brand-new corporation. I'd never heard of the outfit. It's a cover, that's all. But a darned good one. I feel like a puppet on a string!"

Together, they climbed back down to the runway. "Is that the reason you decided to keep Sitting Tight on the job?" Leigh asked. "You said something about our saving you a fortune."

Carlos gave a sheepish laugh. "Anything's worth a try. I figured that if Sentry got *me*, it might catch my nemesis too." He jammed his hands into the pockets of his khakis and leaned back in the shade of his plane. "I admit that your system is quite an invention. Kit Martindale ought to have a brilliant future in front of him. Would you like to tell me a little more about the guy?"

If she and Kit were going to be working with this man, he definitely had the right to do a background check, Leigh reflected. But she had a hunch his concern was personal as well. A few times his gaze had lingered on her with interest, and earlier he had run a hand across the top of her head. He'd stretched out one of the tightly curled ringlets, then let it bounce back into place again.

She rested her shoulders against the fuselage and looked steadily back at him. There was no denying that she found Carlos Wainwright attractive. It would be far too easy to become attached to the man, which really wouldn't be a good idea. She liked her quiet, orderly, semi-successful life the way it was. One of the best things about it was that nowadays no one was walking away and abandoning her. She was safe from that kind of harm so long as she didn't risk her heart.

But she might as well answer his questions and get the background bit over with. That way, she could head back to work and he could forge ahead with his engine repairs. They could stop standing around feeling uncomfortable with each other. If Sitting Tight was going to guard his property, she wanted it to be on a businesslike basis. Darn Roger for going off and leaving her with this dilemma!

"What would you like to know?" she asked. "Kit Martindale is honest, hardworking, and completely dependable. He's a college graduate, he holds patents on a dozen inventions, including Sentry."

"How long have you known him?"

"Since I was seven."

"I take it he was the boy next door?"

"He's the best friend I've ever had." Leigh tilted her chin. "And yes, he did live next door. That was after the bank foreclosed the mortgages on my dad's ranch and we moved into town."

"You and your dad?"

"And DeeDee." The toe of Leigh's shoe swiped at a pebble. "She was my mother."

"Times must have been tough for your family," Carlos said.

"Not at first." She looked away. "It was a prosperous ranch. My father had a feeling for the soil. He loved to see things grow. But he got lonesome out there all by himself, I guess. One time he drove over to Las Vegas for the weekend. He fell head over heels in love with a gorgeous blonde who danced in one of the nightclub revues. Even though she was more than twenty years younger, he talked her into getting married and coming back here to live."

"How did DeeDee like ranch life?"

"Dad tried hard to keep her content by buying her pretty clothes and an expensive car. He got someone to look after me so he could take her on trips to the bright lights. Then she wanted a mink coat, and he bought that too. And lots and lots of cosmetics. She was crazy about them. Perfume, especially. Some of it costs a hundred dollars an ounce, if you can believe such a thing."

Carlos could. He had a luxury-loving younger sister. It was easy to see how those mortgages had come to be foreclosed. He also realized now why it was that Leigh looked so different from all the other girls he knew. Her complexion was mercilessly devoid of makeup. She must have bent over backward to avoid being anything like DeeDee.

"Anyway," she went on, "we moved into town. Kit was a year older than I, the youngest in a family of eight. His folks were used to kids. One more underfoot didn't bother them a bit. Besides, I guess they heard all the yelling over yonder and figured out why I was at their house so often."

"Like having a fallout shelter next door."

Leigh looked at him with respect. He *did* understand. "Very much like that. When I was ten DeeDee ran off with another man and we never saw her again. My father hired on as a day worker when he could. It was hard on him. He wasn't skilled at anything

54

except ranching. But with me to look out for, he couldn't take a steady job on one of the outlying spreads where he might have been able to regain his self-respect. He had to stay in town and take temporary work here and there."

Carlos commented that they had done well to save any money at all toward college.

She hadn't meant to tell him all this. Somehow, it just happened. But she was tired of resisting his questions. Maybe when he learned the rest of it, he'd leave her alone.

"I worked part-time during high school. Dad contributed what he could," Leigh said. "During my freshman year a big story appeared in the newspaper about prospectors finding uranium right here in New Mexico. People were getting rich overnight. Even though he didn't know the first thing about mining, Dad decided that was the way out of our financial difficulties. So he got himself a mule, and a shovel, and a Geiger counter. He asked Kit to please keep on looking out for me, like he always had. And — and he left."

She was finding it hard to keep her voice steady. Tactfully, Carlos watched a couple of roadrunners chase each other around for a minute or two. When she didn't go on, he asked:

"Did he come back?"

"No. Maybe he figured he had done his share."

"So you were left all alone?"

Leigh jerked her head back in surprise. "Why, no. There was Kit. He helped me in every way possible. When my funds finally dribbled out completely, he showed up with a pretty little ring, stuck it on my finger, and said we had better be engaged. That way his folks could take me into their own home between my house-sitting jobs without causing the neighbors' tongues to fall off from wagging."

"I see," Carlos said in a new tone.

"I'm glad you understand why I love Kit so much. And his wife too," Leigh added. "Gail was my favorite classmate. I introduced the two of them. But neither of them would even consider getting married until I graduated and got my company going, and we could dissolve that make-believe engagement with honor." She smiled. "They're so right for each other. So absolutely perfect. They're expecting twins very soon. I'm going to be an aunt!"

So the Martindales were family. At least the closest thing she had to one. In just the brief time he had known her, Carlos was coming to realize that Leigh had a heart filled with love, but practically no one to lavish it on. After being abandoned twice, by each parent in turn, she must be very wary of offering her affection to anyone not willing to cherish it permanently.

But the story of her father's disappearance didn't ring true to him. It seemed out of character. A man who has struggled to do his best for the first eighteen years of his daughter's life doesn't suddenly walk away from her without a backward look.

"Was an official search ever made for your dad?" he asked.

Leigh's face took on a wistful look. "I got terribly worried after not hearing from him for several months. I went down and filed a missing-persons report. His description was circulated around the uranium-mining areas. A couple of deputies checked around, asking questions. No one could remember ever having seen him. Most of the prospectors were loners, of course. They avoided one another and were pretty secretive about any promising spot they might have found."

With darned good reason, Carlos thought. His own recent and frustrating experiences had been a good lesson in that respect. The instance he'd told Leigh about was only the latest claim-jumping episode involving his discoveries. There had been others. Still, it seemed odd that no one out in the hills had even seen her father.

Tumbleweed came dashing up just then, breathless from his attempts to catch up with a jackrabbit. Leigh put her woes aside and giggled at the big mongrel's clumsy antics. She threw her arms around his neck and got a face-licking in return.

"You soft-soaper. Think you're going to get around me, don't you? Well, I don't have any candy in my pocket, so you might as well stop coaxing!" Still laughing, she glanced up to find Carlos watching them with a puzzled frown. "You *did* know that your dog has a voracious craving for sweets, didn't you?"

"Oh, yes. I'm always tempted to loop a tote bag around his neck and let him go out trick-or-treating on Halloween. But with or without lollipops, I don't understand how you won him over. In the past, Tumbleweed has always refused to even stay in the same room with a woman, not even my mother. He snarls and bristles — he's impossible!"

Bewildered, Leigh shrugged. "It's a mystery to me. The first time I talked to her, your secretary claimed he was a female-hating chauvinist. Though I've never done anything special to make friends with Tumbleweed, we've always gotten along just fine."

She straightened up and brushed and plucked long, sandy-colored hair from her pale blue blouse and skirt. "Time for me to get back. Sitting Tight doesn't run itself. Right now I'm matching house-sitters with clients eager to take a fall vacation, and wondering where I can find another dozen reliable employees."

"Don't look at me!" Carlos yanked a wrench out of his pocket to show that his own time was about to be fully occupied.

"Wouldn't dream of it," Leigh assured him. Then she assumed a businesslike attitude. "But I do think the time has come to agree on what needs to be done here. Until now, I've been using that small office near the front hall as my base of operations. Are you certain you want my company to continue keeping an eye on your house?"

"I want it guarded like Fort Knox! Please, Leigh," Carlos added in a softer tone. "I'd really appreciate it if you and Sentry would stick around until I solve the problem of who has been beating me to the punch in identifying and staking out these new oil reserves. And how they're managing it. The dirty work has to be done from this end. All my samples and notes are brought back here. Somehow, those crooks are managing to get a foot in the door and figure out what I've found almost before I realize it myself. I want them caught!"

"We'll do our very best."

Leigh sympathized with his predicament. How terrible to do all that work, then have someone else profit by it!

Her own business needed a minimum of space to be run efficiently. She would have no trouble continuing to operate it from that tiny front cubicle. Practically all her contacts were made by phone. She did mention the advisability of having a separate telephone line installed. At that moment, she was tying up his phone with her numerous routine calls and her answering machine.

"Your family might not understand if they tried to give you a jingle and heard a recorded voice insisting that they had reached a service called Sitting Tight. Worse still," she teased, "what would your girlfriends think?"

"What they've always thought — that there's no accounting for Carlos Wainwright." He grinned, but obviously he was still worried about the subject of their earlier discussion. "It would probably be a good idea to have a second line here in case someone needs to get through in an emergency. Go ahead and fix it up with the phone company. Oh, by the way," he added when she started to turn away, "I haven't forgotten the promise I made last night. The chaperone solution is being taken care of. I got the arrangements underway before you joined me in the kitchen this morning."

"Good!"

She wondered how he meant to solve this particular problem. Fixing it so that they could live under the same roof without causing a breath of gossip was going to be an interesting trick, to say the least.

Most of the day passed without Leigh's curiosity being satisfied. She was just tidying up her papers and rising from the desk to prepare Tumbleweed's dinner when the doorbell chimed.

As usual during the daylight hours when people were in residence, Sentry had been set in its less aggressive "sentinel" mode. Only an attempt at forcible entry would set off the alarm. If the home owner were threatened, however, one touch of a button would immediately summon help without the intruder's realizing that he was about to be apprehended. But such precautions would hardly be needed this time, Leigh saw as soon as she opened the door.

Outside stood four pleasant-faced women. They were clad in the black-and-white habits that had been discontinued except by the most traditional-minded religious orders.

"Good afternoon," one of the nuns said. "I hope we have come to the right address. Mother Superior said that lodgings had been found for us here during the weeks we'll be visiting in Santa Fe. Our schoolteachers from all over the state are here to take advantage of the refresher courses in Native American languages being offered through the Mission."

"That's terrific. Wonderful. Uh, won't you come in?" Trying to hide her surprise, Leigh ushered the sisters into the living room. "Please, make yourselves comfortable," she invited. "I'll go find your host. I'm sure he will want to welcome you in person before I show you to the guest quarters."

She backed out of the room and headed outside in a hurry. His girlfriends were right, she thought. There *was* no accounting for Carlos Wainwright. When he promised to find an impeccable *duenna* for a girl, he didn't settle for half measures!

Chapter Four

An hour later, with the nuns now settled comfortably in the guest wing, Carlos was still amused. Leigh's reaction to his bombshell had been worth waiting for.

"The Mother Superior at one of the local convents is my Aunt Carmelita," he explained. "During the summer, sisters travel to Santa Fe from all over the Southwest to attend these Indian language courses at the Mission. Consequently, lodgings are at a premium. This morning I called up and volunteered the use of my spare rooms instead of waiting to be petitioned. Tia Carmelita was very pleased."

"I'm very pleased too. You've solved our problem beautifully. But you might have tipped me off to what you were planning."

His eyes twinkled. "Then you probably would have accused me of bragging about being a do-gooder. Besides, I wouldn't have gotten to see that flabbergasted look on your face!"

Carlos added that the nuns had a rigorous schedule. Very seldom in past years, when they were in residence, had his path crossed with theirs. He finished: "But the mere fact that they are sharing the house with us will certainly eliminate any raised eyebrows. Better teach them how to get along with Sentry."

Leigh nodded. "I'm not surprised that the language courses are so popular," she observed. "Here in New Mexico alone there are dozens of Indian dialects. Schoolteachers in outlying regions really have to be linguists, especially since they're often transferred from one part of the state to another."

Carlos agreed that communicating with rural people could be quite a problem. His profession took him to a variety of sparsely populated regions. Now and then, he'd found that a familiarity with a basic vocabulary in several different tongues came in mighty handy. In North America, he said, the hundreds of distinct Indian languages were grouped into fifty language families based on similarities in grammar. Then these groups were clustered into six vast superfamilies. The dialects spoken by the various New Mexican tribes all fell within the Aztec-Tanoan superfamily of languages.

"But a Pueblo Indian's vocabulary would still be Greek to a Zunian," he went on. "Each of them would still have to learn a whole new system to hold a discussion."

"Good thing the languages are so economical," Leigh said. "One word in an Indian tongue often takes the place of a whole phrase in English."

When Carlos remarked that that observation sounded as if it came from experience, Leigh nodded. "When I was little, our housekeeper on the ranch told me bedtime stories in the Jemez tongue," she said. "Then, after we moved into town, I had a close friend in grammar school who'd come from the San Ildefonso Pueblo. She taught me the Tewa dialect so that I could talk with her grandmother. And of course I took Spanish in high school, though most kids growing up in Santa Fe seem to pick that up by osmosis, anyway."

He himself had grown up completely bilingual, Carlos said. His ease with Spanish had helped to advance his career. Without it, he couldn't have won the assignment to help explore and test parts of the Yucatán region for a major international oil company.

"I wondered about your name," Leigh admitted. "Carlos is totally Hispanic, while Wainwright could hardly be more Anglo."

"My mother's forebears arrived in the New World from Spain in 1599, twenty years or more before the *Mayflower* set sail across the Atlantic," he told her proudly. "Some of them were later massacred in the Indian uprising led by Popé. With all the other settlers, the survivors were temporarily driven down into El Paso. But they came north again in a few years, made peace with all the Indians, and eventually helped to blaze the famous Santa Fe Trail."

"Your dad's people, on the other hand. . . ."

"They were from Arizona." Carlos laughed. "My mother broke with tradition in a big way by marrying an Anglo. She's never been sorry, though. She and my father have had an extremely happy marriage."

Carlos seemed comfortable with himself, Leigh thought. Perhaps the blend of bloodlines had something to do with that. Early on, he would have had to learn to steer a middle course between two very different cultures. "Is he a geologist?"

"No, he's a dowser. For generations back, my father's ancestors have had the talent of finding water where nobody else could. He inherited the knack and improved on it by combining science with instinct. Some of the techniques I use in looking for oil are spin-offs from methods he taught me."

His parents were currently in Australia,

Carlos added. The government there had contracted with Samuel Wainwright to help locate and develop irrigation sources in the arid Outback. His older sister, Ines, was married to an airline captain. They and their two sons lived in Anchorage, Alaska.

"You can see how I got stuck with the job of keeping an eye on Serita. My little sister is only twenty."

Carlos said that until recently she had worked as an interpreter and translator for a Dallas firm that imported goods from Chile, Argentina, and Brazil. Then, he added grimly, she had met a man.

"This Denny Cahill seems to have swept her off her feet. All she talks about anymore is some new process he has developed for pumping oil out of the ground faster than a conventional rig can do it. She wants to start a partnership with him, and go into full-scale production of the machinery as soon as she turns twenty-one this fall."

That, he added with a touch of cynicism, was when she would come into the inheritance their grandfather had left her in his will. Leigh could tell he was troubled not only about his sister's chancy business plans but also about the man she had decided to marry. A little tactful probing on her part elicited the information that Denny Cahill was more than fifteen years older than Serita. On top of that, he had been married before.

"To an heiress," Carlos said gloomily. "I've heard more than one person claim that Jimmi Haviland settled a good chunk of money on the guy just to get rid of him."

Leigh raised her eyebrows. Gossip columns didn't interest her much, but even she had heard of the extravagant and beautiful playgirl. If Serita's boyfriend moved with that crowd, he was far more likely to be a playboy than a serious businessman. Then she chided herself for making snap judgments. People *did* change. Chances were that Denny Cahill had turned over a new leaf and was working hard to make a success of the pump he had developed.

"I imagine your sister won't listen to a word against him?"

"Not a syllable," Carlos confirmed her guess. "I really hate playing the part of the bossy big brother. Cahill and I met when I flew down for a visit at Easter. He was hearty and delighted to meet me. Too much so, I thought. But how can you criticize something like that to a girl who considers him the man of her dreams?"

"Sounds mighty hard to do," Leigh said. "Especially if he appears to have plenty of money and isn't after hers so obviously that it shows. At least he seems determined to get along with his future in-laws."

"Believe it or not, he seems to be looking forward to having me as a brother-in-law. He crawled all over my plane on that visit. Anyone would have thought it was a Lear jet, he made such a fuss. He even asked if I'd consider giving him flying lessons.

His mention of the little aircraft reminded Leigh of the mechanical problems he had spent the day trying to solve. "Did you get your repairs finished?"

"To be positive, I'll have to wait till the next time I go up. If I get back down safely, I'll know it's okay."

Although Carlos had been joking, he regretted the quip as soon as he heard Leigh's quick intake of breath. She had paled a little, and freckles stood out across the bridge of her nose.

Quickly he covered her hand with his own. His other hand rose and caressed her hair. For some reason, his fingers enjoyed getting lost in those springy ringlets.

"I'm sorry. I apologize. Comes from listening to those daredevil crop dusters I run into at commercial hangars. Some of their bravado must have rubbed off. But I never meant to give you the idea I take stupid chances. I don't."

Leigh was almost more stunned by her reaction than he had been. In the past twenty-four hours she had come to regard Carlos Wainwright as a solid citizen. Dependable. Someone you could count on to do the right thing. His glib remark about safe landings seemed totally out of sync for him.

"I'm sure glad to hear that," she said, realizing how contrite he was for having upset her. "Everything I've seen and heard about you so far made me feel certain you'd be careful about things like maintenance. For example, the way your house and grounds are kept up." Even his lithe, hard-muscled body. Leigh swallowed hard as the thought crossed her mind. But it was true. He took care of the things he owned, and of himself too.

"I *am* careful, Leigh. I can't afford not to be. Not if I intend to become an indulgent old grandfather someday, as I certainly do."

Carlos wondered suddenly what Leigh's future children would look like. They'd probably inherit that cute, upturned nose. As hastily as he had brought it up there, he took his hand away from her hair and moved back a few inches on the sofa. She looked relieved, he noticed, and he became aware that he'd been crowding her without meaning to. But he had been so touched. She really had seemed to care about his safety.

"My oil-pressure gauge started acting up on this last trip home." He wanted to explain the trouble to her so she'd see there was no cause for worry. "This afternoon I cleaned it thoroughly, blew out all the hydraulic lines, and ran the engine for a while to make sure it was back up to par. The problem was probably caused by a speck of dirt. At any rate, it seems to be performing just fine now."

His assurances made Leigh feel a whole lot better. She wondered what had come over her a few minutes earlier. Usually, she was so unflappable. Two years back, a freak tornado had zipped through town and taken off part of the roof of the house where she'd been sitting. She'd called for emergency help, then efficiently set about moving books and pictures out of harm's way. Yet a minute ago, the mere notion of Carlos's experiencing mid-air engine trouble had left her sick with apprehension.

"Do you think the gauge will be all right for your trip to Texas?" she asked with concern.

"Yes, I do. But to be absolutely sure, I'm going to take the plane over to Oklahoma City first to deliver my report on the Yucatán exploration. That isn't far as the crow flies, and I'll set a course that will avoid the worst of the mountain."

West of Santa Fe were the high peaks of the Sangre de Cristo Mountains. Nevertheless, Carlos knew that by angling somewhat in a southerly direction he could avoid much increase in altitude and avoid crossing the vast, lonely regions that the trip to Texas would necessitate.

He explained this reasoning very carefully to Leigh. Within a few minutes she was her normal, cheerful self again. Leaving him in his office to begin outlining his report, she went off for a just-before-bedtime romp with Tumbleweed.

"You'd sure make it easier for both of us if you didn't always insist on avoiding the garden," she grumbled, trudging back from their hike across the open fields. But on that point Tumbleweed was adamant. He refused to go anywhere near the carefully tended flower garden.

It was nice of Carlos to set her mind at ease by telling her about the shakedown flight he intended to make to test the balky gauge. He probably thought she was scared of her own shadow. In truth, she was a fairly courageous person. She just wanted him to stay safe.

★ ★ ★

The next few days were completely un-eventful. Carlos spent his time plowing through reams of notes taken in Mexico, making sure the report he compiled was perfect. Leigh made a trip into town to interview the manager of a heating and air-condition-ing firm that Kit had recommended she try. She put the company on a retainer. Should one of the houses under Sitting Tight's care develop a problem with its temperature con-trols, a serviceman from the firm would promptly take care of the matter.

She also spent some time with the nuns who were using the Wainwright home as their base. They were fascinated by Sentry, and quick to learn how to manipulate the inside control panel. But they declined in-structions on how to neutralize the protective device from outside.

"We have too much homework to do to be running around at night," Sister Ber-nadette said. "And we've been practicing our vocabularies aloud to see if we can at least learn to understand one another."

"It seems so funny to hear teachers talk about doing homework," Leigh said with a laugh.

"Yes, I'm sure our students would think so too," Sister Mary Jude agreed. "But these courses will save us a great deal of trial and error later, and hopefully help us reach a child who can't communicate any other way except in his own dialect. Some of the pueblos are terribly remote. The elders may speak English or Spanish, but chances are that the women and children don't. When we're sent out to start up a little school in the backcountry, we need all the extra pluses we can get."

Like the nuns, Leigh's own path didn't cross with Carlos's all the time. Each of them had work to do. However, one morning he paused in the doorway of her small office. Occupied by playing back the tape on her answering machine, she didn't notice him at first. Her head was bent over a notebook while she jotted memos on a page. One message ended. Another began. Hearing the too-familiar voice, Leigh sighed.

"Boss, this is Angelina," the caller announced. "You know, I think the Stuarts deliberately wait until every single thing in their house is ready to self-destruct. Then they hire us and leave on vacation. So far, Pete has been out to fix the dishwasher, Herman Running Deer came and tinkered with the circuit breakers, the philodendron died and had to be replaced, Diego spent two hours repairing the sprinkler system out front, and even the flea collar on their darned itchy cat was a year out of date. Next time they apply for a house-sitter, I suggest —"

A slight movement in the doorway caught Leigh's attention. She glanced up to see Carlos wearing an ear-to-ear grin. Stabbing an index finger at the answering machine, she cut off Angelina in mid-recommendation.

"Angelina's vocabulary tends to be a little indelicate for mixed company," she said. That was an understatement. The outspoken science major could give griping lessons to a protest group. But she was reliable, and so it balanced out.

"How's everything, Carlos?"

"Not too bad, actually. The report needs only a couple of finishing touches and it's complete. I have an appointment to deliver it to the committee at eleven tomorrow morning." He came into the room and perched on a corner of her desk. "I was wondering whether you might like to go out to dinner with me tonight. Help me celebrate being done with this job at last. I'm looking forward to finishing up my contract and going back to exploring on my own."

"Thanks, I'd love to go," Leigh said. "And I understand your feelings about working for yourself at your own pace. I enjoy running my own business, even though there are times when it seems about to grow out of hand. If the demand keeps up, I may have to hire an office assistant."

But that, she added, would mean renting larger business quarters. She loved her little cubbyhole downtown, overlooking the old Palace of the Governors. "From my one and only window I can look out at all those reminders of Santa Fe's history. Buildings by the Spaniards, parks by the Anglos, the Indians selling their jewelry down in the Plaza. . . ."

Like Carlos, she thought, the town was a compatible mix of diverse cultures.

He confided that one of his favorite restaurants lay just north of the town on the Old Taos Highway. "Wonderful Mexican food, and the guitar music is enough to really stir up your blood."

Leigh lowered her eyes. The man sitting chummily on the edge of her desk was quite capable of stirring up her blood all by himself. She didn't need the extra stimulation of romantic music to start her wondering what, if anything, lay ahead for them.

"I know the place you mean," she told him. "It tends to be pretty dressy. Maybe I'll drive over to my apartment this afternoon and see what I can find in my closet." Her house-sitting wardrobe, she added as she offered to make the dinner reservations, ran strictly to sports clothes. "What time shall I say we'll be there?"

"Seven? It's early, I know, but I have a long checklist to run through before taking off tomorrow morning."

Later that day, Leigh straightened up her desk and called in to Carlos, saying that she'd be back in an hour or so. Then she hopped into her two-year-old white Ford Mustang and headed home.

The pink adobe apartment building where she lived was situated near the center of Santa Fe. When the narrow, winding streets were laid out hundreds of years ago, they were built to accommodate burro carts and *caballeros,* gentlemen on horseback. Parking was difficult. Horrendous traffic jams had been known to result if an unknowing tourist in a large motor home took the wrong turn, then found himself unable to back around.

Leigh squeezed her Mustang as close to the curb as possible and climbed out. Cottonwoods shaded her building. Their leafy presence made a cool difference during the breathless, sunbaked afternoon. But she knew that as soon as the sun went down, the temperature would drop. She reminded herself to bring a jacket along. At seven thousand feet above sea level, Santa Fe could grow decidedly chilly even on midsummer nights.

She showered and scrubbed her hair until it squeaked. After toweling it vigorously, she flipped the damp ringlets around her fingers with a comb to arrange them in place. Soon she was slipping her favorite pima-cotton dress over her head.

Its creator, a local designer, had left the parchment-colored fabric undyed. The scooped neckline and short sleeves were edged with soft beige yarn, and the fitted bodice nipped in at the waist. The design on the full skirt was what made the dress so special. It had been hand-embroidered with the red and yellow sun emblems that had originated centuries before in the Zia pueblo. In modern times the symbol decorated New Mexico's state flag, officially representing the Land of Enchantment.

Turquoise and silver earrings and a matching bracelet complemented the outfit. Sheer nylons and pretty, high-heeled pumps added a note of sophistication as well as a few inches of height.

Studying her reflection, Leigh decided that she looked trim, well dressed, and immaculately groomed. Yet, for the first time in her life, she was conscious of something lacking. She felt sure that the girls Carlos usually dated must be far more glamorous than she. And more colorful. To his eyes, she was bound to appear very plain.

With a sigh, she turned away from the dressing table and picked up her jacket. The clock on her nightstand told her it was still quite early.

There'd be time, plenty of time, if she really wanted to add . . . anything.

Emerging from the building, she started toward her car, and then hesitated. Suddenly resolute, she turned around and headed instead toward the corner drugstore. Ten minutes later she came out again. The bag she carried contained an assortment of small items. Leigh slipped in behind the wheel. Reaching up, she tilted the rearview mirror and gave her face one last chance to measure up on its own.

After a sober, unbiased appraisal, she reluctantly conceded that her first impression had been the right one. She *was* plain, Leigh thought as she reached toward the sack on the seat beside her. Hopefully, she could manage to get some of this stuff on without smearing it all over her skin.

First, from a pale pink tube, gloss was dabbed sparingly across her lips. That wasn't too awful, Leigh decided. Next, she experimented with a light frosting of blue eye shadow. A film of ebony mascara was carefully applied along the length of her thickly fringed lashes.

Gazing back at her now was the face of a stranger, a magazine girl and not Leigh Sinclair at all. Just someone prettied up for the glossies.

One last item remained to be opened. This particular brand of perfume was advertised everywhere. Top models seemed to swear by it. Leigh stared distastefully at the crystal vial, then shrugged and broke the seal. *Go for broke,* she thought.

Dabbing drops of the fragrance onto her wrists and behind her ears, she made a strong effort not to breathe in the floral scent. It didn't work, however, and all at once she was a small girl again, watching a beautiful blond woman making up her face, and scattering cosmetics carelessly across the dressing table, and talking about the stage — what a hit she'd been, and how she wished she were back in Vegas.

Fragrance, heavy and cloying, had floated suffocatingly through that elegant bedroom. And DeeDee had sat there in her satin dressing gown, painting her long, oval nails.

With an angry gesture, Leigh thrust the cosmetics back into the bag. Unceremoniously, she jammed the parcel into her glove compartment. A moment later she had re-adjusted the rearview mirror so as not to have to look at the stranger reflected there, and she was headed out on the now-familiar route.

She had done her level best — or worst. But if Carlos still wasn't satisfied with her appearance, he had only to say so. She'd be glad to break their date. Let him invite someone else out. She would go and have a pizza. Maybe Tumbleweed would like to share it with her.

This notion snapped her out of the bleak mood. What in the world was she fussing about? Carlos was bound to think she looked terrific.

Leigh was feeling almost cheerful again by the time she entered the house. The sisters had already finished their early dinner. They were enjoying a radio program of classical music while preparing to settle down with their language studies for the evening. Leigh called out a good night to them, then turned down the hall toward the kitchen, where it was time to feed Tumbleweed.

Carlos had apparently had the same thought, and was there ahead of her. A few steps short of the door, Leigh heard the whirr of the electric can opener and an eager, hungry bark.

It was a delightful, homey scene she stepped into. The dark, attractive man turned toward her with a smile. The tail-wagging dog pranced around.

Then he snarled. Ferociously. It was clear that he was hungry, Leigh thought, suddenly afraid. The big mutt had stiffened. His hair stood on end. His massive body was poised to leap as he confronted her with bared teeth.

She felt like an hors d'oeuvre about to be snapped up!

Chapter Five

Carlos slammed the can of pet food he'd been opening onto the counter. In astonishment, he made a grab for the dog's collar. "Tumbleweed! What ails you?"

The only response he received was a low, threatening growl. Baffled, he squatted down beside the animal. Smoothing back the ruffled fur, he spoke in a quiet, reassuring tone: "Take it easy, buddy. No need to get your hackles up. I thought you'd finally outgrown that woman-hating act you used to put on." He glanced over at Leigh, who had retreated to the doorway. "I don't get it. Just this morning he was cavorting around with the nuns, as frisky as you please. All four of them were taking turns petting him."

"Well, *they* might still be on his good side, but he sure seems to have changed his mind about *me!*" Tears blurred her eyes. She hadn't felt so rejected in years, not since her father had walked away never to return.

"I sure can't figure you out." Carlos sounded ashamed of his dog's unfriendly behavior. "Half the time you act as if you like her better than me. Now look at you!"

Leigh hated to see Tumbleweed scolded. The big mongrel kept swinging his head from one to the other of them. Between snarls, his whine sounded piteous. Some invisible demon seemed to be prodding him. "I don't believe he knows what the trouble is himself," she said.

"See that puzzled expression in his eyes?"

"Uh-huh. Darn it, Leigh, there *has* to be a logical explanation. He was fine up until a minute ago. Then you came in."

Determined to unravel the mystery even if it took all night, Carlos gave Leigh a long, appraising look. As always, she looked scrumptuous, but more dressed up than usual because they had a dinner date. Then his gaze narrowed. Still perplexed, it dawned on him that there was something different about her. Did she generally wear lip gloss and eye shadow?

Just then, a waft of expensive perfume undulated past his nose. *That* was something new, he'd lay odds on it!

"Wait a minute!" he exclaimed. "I've got a hunch it isn't you personally he's objecting to, Leigh. You never wore makeup or perfume around him before, did you?"

"I never wore it around anyone before!" And she wished to heaven that she hadn't thought of doing so this time, either. "But why should your dog be having conniptions over this muck on my face?"

Her words were a dead giveaway, and Carlos felt a tug at his heartstrings. She must have bought the cosmetics especially to wear that evening. He hadn't forgotten the poignant tale of her past, of her brief-as-possible sketch of the mother who had taken more interest in frills, makeup, and perfume than in her own child. Ordinarily, he felt sure, Leigh went out of her way to shun DeeDee's favorite luxuries. But to-night, because he had asked her out, she had given in against her better judgment. Maybe she had thought that he preferred the glossy look.

Carlos swallowed, amazed at the sudden rush of sentiment. She couldn't guess how appealing he found her natural beauty, her loveliness that went all the way through to her soul. And how hurt she must be by that idiot dog's weird reaction!

Straightening up, he grabbed the can of food and emptied it into the big blue dish. Then, using the savory stew as a lure, he coaxed Tumbleweed into the pantry, set the meal down in front of the confused animal, and rapidly closed the door.

"I don't know what his problem is, but if

we think it over rationally, we can figure it out."

As Carlos walked over to Leigh his warm brown eyes traveled appreciatively across her. "It's going to be a pleasure to take you out and show you off to the town," he said. "To tell the truth, though, I was looking forward to holding a hundred percent girl in my arms instead of someone who's part Lily Vanderglitz or whatever that brand of makeup is called."

He was close enough for her to reach out and brush the sleeve of his jacket. Another step, Leigh thought, and she would be in his arms. A wan smile crossed her face at his fanciful reference to those expensive cosmetics she'd splurged on. "Do you really think I look okay without it?"

"You're beautiful, Leigh. I've always thought so. Even that first night, when you were standing here in your bare feet, hauling away at Tumbleweed's leash and trying to keep him from gnawing on a housebreaker."

A radiant glow lit her face. His sincere compliment made her feel so wonderful that it was actually a little frightening. She was fond of a number of people. There were even a few, like Kit and Gail, whom she truly loved. But this . . . this was a new sensation. She was drawn to take that last step forward, to let him know of her feelings.

But a sudden shyness caused her to move back a few inches instead. In confusion, she glanced at the closed pantry door. If Tumbleweed had a valid reason for his behavior, she wouldn't feel half so demoralized. For her own peace of mind she'd have to try and find out what it was. But there was something else she needed to do first.

"Would you excuse me for a minute, Carlos?"

Just a door down the hall was her own room. Leigh headed for its adjacent bath. After a quick but thorough session with soap and water, she felt much more like her normal self. There was nothing wrong with makeup. It simply wasn't for her. She hoped she would never again be foolish enough to try something that went completely against her grain merely because other people favored it.

Carlos's assurances had given her morale a terrific boost. Someday, she might be able to tell him how very much she appreciated his put-down of Lily Vanderglitz.

When she returned to the kitchen, his genuine smile let her know that he hadn't just been talking to make her feel better. He really did seem to find the unvarnished Leigh Sinclair preferable to the one gilded by Lily.

"You look great," he said. "That dress is a knockout, and so is that just-scrubbed complexion. Ready to try an experiment?"

She nodded, resisting the urge to poise for flight. "Yes, if you think we have time."

"I phoned and put back our dinner reservations a half hour," Carlos told her. "Then I did some deep thinking. I believe I've figured out the problem. If I'm right, you'll have done everyone an enormous favor by pulling a switch on that mixed-up dog. Let's see what he thinks of you now."

Leigh braced herself for the encounter. The precaution turned out to be unnecessary. Tumbleweed stuck his head around the corner of the pantry, casting a cautious look in her direction. A little yelp rumbled from his throat. This time, though, he seemed to be voicing a welcome. At once he trotted across the room to nuzzle the hand she held out to him.

"Good boy!" Leigh cried out in relief. "You must have really hated the makeup."

"Actually, I think it was the perfume," Carlos said.

"But the scent wasn't that heavy. It was just a delicate, flowery fragrance."

"You've said the key word — 'flower.' " Carlos patted the dog, smoothing his fur to show there were no hard feelings. "I never told you how this silly mongrel and I happened to team up, did I?"

"No. I just figured the two of you came as a set."

Leigh listened with interest while Carlos explained how he had happened across the small, forlorn puppy in the desert a couple of years ago. "I had been doing some rock testing, and carelessly neglected to keep an eye on the weather. A fierce sandstorm blew up. It caught me by surprise about a half mile from where I'd set the plane down."

He had prudently stayed put, clinging for dear life to a big, rough boulder rather than trying to find his way back in the teeth of that howling wind. When the storm finally abated and he could think of something besides bare survival again, he became aware of a desperate whimpering in a nearby patch of foliage.

"There was Tumbleweed. I have no idea where he'd come from, but the poor little guy had been blown into a bush that was literally covered with thorns. His fur was all tangled up in those needle-sharp stickers. He must have been trapped there for hours, hemmed in by brambles and big white flowers. They had a cloying, potent smell something like gardenia."

Leigh wrinkled her nose. Gardenias always

gave her a headache. "No wonder that even today he's so sensitive to fragrances. Oh! That must be why he always insists on heading for the open countryside for his evening walk. He won't even go near the courtyard flower garden."

Carlos felt negligent for never having realized before that pets as well as people might sometimes be prone to allergies. He said with a grin, "I'll have to spread the word around to my family and friends that Tumbleweed isn't a woman-hater, after all. Just like any normal male, he's really crazy about girls. But the perfumy way most of them smell brings back such unhappy memories for him that he can't stand to be around them. No wonder he's so partial to you and the nuns."

With the mystery solved, they settled the genial dog down for the evening and hastened out to the garage. This was the first time Leigh had ridden in the flame-red Pontiac GTA. Along with his plane, the Trans-Am was Carlos's pride and joy. The speedometer on the aerodynamically engineered car showed a top capability of one hundred forty miles per hour. On the traffic-free road, he pushed the pedal to the metal, shooting the needle more than halfway up.

Leaning back in the comfortable bucket

seat, held securely by her shoulder harness, Leigh gazed up through the transparent T-Top and watched the clouds roll overhead. They seemed to be preparing for a vivid sunset.

"What a great car!" she exclaimed. "But I'd just as soon you weren't barreling along at this speed."

Carlos smiled and slowed down.

Even in midweek the restaurant they had chosen was extremely crowded. After they were conducted to a very private table, screened off from other diners by bowers of exotic greenery, Carlos asked what sort of aperitif she would like. "Generally, I like a glass of wine before dinner," he said. "But a long time ago I made it a rule never to have anything alcoholic to drink within twenty-four hours of a flight where I'll be handling the controls."

This policy sounded highly sensible to Leigh. With him, she opted for tomato juice with a squeeze of lemon while considering the rest of the menu. Over piquantly spiced salad, they discussed his forthcoming trip to Oklahoma City.

"I'm sure glad to be finishing up this session of contract work," Carlos said. "It's a lot more challenging to explore on my own than fly around in a quadrant, mapping out someone else's field."

"Must be great experience, though."

"Sure. I'm always picking up useful tips on what to keep my eyes open for. How to double-check coordinates, and what to do when I spot a promising outcrop that might indicate oil somewhere deep in the strata below."

As his expression grew more reserved, Leigh suspected that he was thinking of the mysterious thefts of his recent discoveries. So far, he hadn't had the slightest bit of luck in figuring out how the piracy could have been accomplished.

She was enchanted to hear the mellow twanging of strings. Strolling guitarists dressed in mariachi costumes serenaded each table in turn. Carlos folded Leigh's hand inside his own, then leaned back to enjoy the traditional Latin favorites.

For the main course they had ordered chili *rellenos*. These were eight-inch-long pepper pods stuffed with a mixture of cheddar and goat-milk *asadero* cheese. The plump, mild chilis were then batter dipped and deep fried. Served with white rice and mashed refried beans sprinkled with more cheese, the dish was utterly delicious.

Between bites, Leigh asked if Carlos knew how to navigate by the stars or whether he depended on dead reckoning in addition to his aircraft's inertial guidance system.

He replied that he used all three methods, depending on the circumstances. "Celestial navigation is handy to know because it will help you tell the direction whether you're in the air, on the ground, or even out at sea far from land. And it's a godsend if you are up in an airplane and your compass suddenly goes haywire."

On the other hand, Carlos said, navigating by the stars could be extremely complicated. "As the Earth orbits through space, the constellations seem to change positions constantly. Time of night, time of year — it all makes a difference. And our old familiar guidelines here in Santa Fe would be of little help in going from Argentina to Chile, say. Each hemisphere has its own set of stars."

Leigh learned that his plane had a number of mechanical aids to navigation, as finding one's way around the sky was sometimes called.

Carlos laughingly referred to dead reckoning as the art of following one's nose. "Flying by the seat of your pants, as the old barnstormers used to call it. Educated guesswork."

"Educated" would be the watchword, she suspected. It probably took years of training and experience to know what to look for.

Thinking of the way he bounced around the planet, she wished suddenly that she could fly too, to soar above the ordinariness of her life just for once. Even Kit, her dearest friend, occasionally commented on her tendency to play it safe, to avoid taking chances. Caution was fine, he agreed, but never daring to try one's wings was hardly a way to find happiness. Yet look what had happened this evening, when she had conquered a lifelong aversion to cosmetics. She'd darned near been eaten!

It undoubtedly had something to do with the insecurity of her childhood, and the fact that first one parent and then the other had turned their backs and walked out on her. Whatever the cause, she knew herself to be too prudent. *You're a stick-in-the mud,* she castigated herself gloomily. Compared to the adventures that colored the lives of others, everything about her was prosaic and dull. Roger MacKenzie might never run across the Seven Cities of Cibola, yet the very search added excitement to an otherwise dull existence. She, on the other hand, held back from venturing out into the unknown, especially when it came to risking her heart.

What she needed, Leigh lectured herself,

was a vacation. And soon. When the busy summer season was over, she'd delegate the office management and go. She would learn to — to surf, or something. And have a good time. She would!

She felt a little foolish as these thoughts popped into her head. She was usually a cheerful person, and wondered if this un-characteristic dejection might not have something to do with the fact that Carlos was leaving in the morning. She reminded herself that he planned only a short business trip. As soon as the scheduled conference in Oklahoma City was over, he'd be back. At least temporarily. But then . . . ?

Carlos also seemed to have lapsed into his own thoughts. A few times Leigh glanced up to find him looking at her intently. She wondered what he could be thinking. To get the conversation started again, she mentioned a TV miniseries they had both watched with enjoyment that week. Carlos seized on the topic gratefully. Maybe, she thought, he had also been wondering what to say next.

Before she knew it, their entrées had disappeared and dinner plates were being exchanged for dessert dishes. Lighter-than-air pastries, *sopaipilla* strips, were set in front of them, accompanied by a chocolate, cinnamon-flavored *champura* sauce.

"We'll be waddling out!" But in spite of this groan, Leigh devoted herself to the delicious sweet, sipped every drop of her coffee, and had to bite her tongue to keep from asking for seconds.

"That was wonderful," she told Carlos on the way home. She noticed that he was keeping his car under the speed limit this time, and she wondered whether a little of her innate caution might be rubbing off on him.

He had certainly learned to cope very efficiently with Sentry. Leigh watched him manipulate the correct set of buttons, remembering how he had gotten the worst of it the first time he'd encountered the security system.

As usual, Tumbleweed was ecstatic at having company, and he prevailed on them both to escort him outside for a pre-bedtime ramble. It wasn't until they had brought the dog back inside the courtyard that Leigh realized that Carlos was awfully quiet.

He'd paused near the gate and was watching her. "You'll be all right here alone, won't you?"

"Well, of course!" Leigh was surprised, and a little touched at his concern. "Besides,

I'm not alone. There's Tumbleweed and the nuns. Not to mention Sentry."

"How could I have overlooked Sentry?" His lips formed a wry curve. "And in addition to everything else, you're used to taking care of people's houses and seeing that nothing goes wrong. So I don't have any cause to worry, right?"

She nodded. "Right."

"I'll miss you, anyway."

He reached out, taking her by the elbows. Leigh could feel herself being drawn closer. Rather flustered, she raised her hands to smooth out a little fold in his shirt collar. But no matter how slowly her fingers moved, she couldn't procrastinate more than a few seconds. After that, she had no further excuse for not looking up.

Raising her eyes, she saw that his faint smile had faded. In the shadows, his face looked still and intent.

"We . . . we haven't known each other very long," she said.

"No. Sometimes it doesn't take very long."

Her dad had met and married DeeDee all in the same weekend, Leigh recalled. She pushed the unwelcome thought aside. A moment later she was lost in the warmth and tenderness of Carlos's embrace. His arms shut out the evening chill. His kiss made her feel needed, cared for, and very, very special.

He was right. Sometimes it didn't take very long.

Chapter Six

"No, I'm sorry. He isn't here at the moment. Would you care to leave a message?"

"Oh, what a bother!" a young, exuberant voice exclaimed. "I needed to talk with him direct. You must be pinch-hitting for Brenda. I heard that she flew back to Chicago to help her mother through the recuperation period."

In resignation, Leigh penciled a mark in her ledger so as not to lose track of how far down the column her calculator's figures currently covered. Bookkeeping was far from her favorite activity, and she had been hoping to compile the July totals this morning. That way, all of the previous month's accounts would be complete and off her mind. But monitoring an absent home owner's phone calls was a normal part of house-sitting. She had no right to resent the interruption.

"That's right," she said. "Brenda Tucker is still back East. But I haven't taken over her secretarial duties. I'm only house-sitting while Mr. Wainwright is out of town."

"Oh!" the girl said. Her clear, forceful

voice faded a little as she must have turned her head to speak with someone in the same room with her. "Carlos is away. The person who answered says she's the house-sitter."

A man's voice rumbled in the background. His words were a drawling, indistinct blur, but Leigh detected a note of annoyance.

"Well, I can't help it," the girl said to the man. "He said he would come down when he could take a few days off again. He was just here at Easter. What do you expect me to do — ask a complete stranger if she thinks my brother might agree to advance me part of my inheritance three months early?"

Leigh's eyebrows lifted. Serita was talking to her fiancé, the man Carlos viewed with such misgivings. Though their affairs were none of her business, she couldn't help feeling that Carlos might very well have good reason for suspecting the worst. It sounded to her as if Denny Cahill couldn't wait to get his hands on his future wife's money.

Sitting Tight's accounts were completely forgotten, and Leigh continued to listen with interest to the squabble on the other end of the line. She didn't consider this eavesdropping. If the engaged couple didn't have sense enough to argue in private, they deserved to be overheard. In fact, she felt inclined to cheer the fight on. If the quarrel reached the recriminations stage, Serita might get an eye-opening notion of what her fiancé was really interested in.

It didn't go that far, however. The girl's voice became distinct and courteous again as she once more brought the receiver close to her mouth.

"This is Serita Wainwright speaking. I was wondering if you might have some idea of my brother's schedule. Do you expect him back soon?"

"Within a few days, I believe." Leigh had not been authorized to disclose Carlos's whereabouts, although she would have done so in an emergency. "If you'll give me your phone number, I'll make a note and ask him to return your call as soon as he arrives home."

"I guess I'll have to settle for that." Serita sighed theatrically and provided the information.

Leigh shook her head as she hung up. Carlos certainly had had his share of problems lately. Plane trouble, worries about some mysterious corporation beating him to the claims office, and now this heavy responsibility for his younger sister. From what she had overheard, he had good cause to be concerned. It sounded very much as if Denny Cahill was far more interested in money than in his fiancée.

But it probably was unfair to judge them on the strength of one spat. Maybe it was Serita who was eager to start spending her inheritance. She sounded plenty headstrong. Leigh remembered herself a few years back, refusing advice, insisting on doing things her own way, right or wrong. And a good part of the time, she *had* been wrong. Like everyone else, she'd had to learn from experience. Serita would too. For the other girl's sake, she hoped that the experience wouldn't prove to be too harsh. At twenty or at any other time in one's life, it was a crushing blow to discover that people didn't really love you, after all.

Shifting restlessly in her chair, Leigh recalled her decision to take a vacation. Yesterday evening, when she was feeling so morose about Carlos going away, she had half-convinced herself that she needed a change of pace and some new scenery. But in her heart she knew this wasn't so. She loved Santa Fe, enjoyed her job, and hadn't the faintest desire to go off on a tour or a cruise.

Carlos, on the other hand, was an adventurous person. He was forever flying off someplace or other. What was really scaring her, Leigh conceded, was the worry that they might be falling in love in spite of having so little in common. That was what had happened to her parents — a quick courtship, then disaster! They had fought for the next decade, and finally DeeDee walked away without a backward look.

Leigh knew she would be incapable of ever doing a thing like that. She was the steady one, the reliable businesswoman, in a rut as deep as the Grand Canyon. Nevertheless, if she fell as deeply in love with Carlos Wainwright as she feared herself in danger of doing, mightn't she be risking a lifetime of unhappiness? What if he thought he was in love with her too, then decided she was too dull and unexciting to suit him over the long haul?

Elbows propped on the desk, chin sunk in her hands, she pondered her situation. Should she get away and think things over? Then her eye fell on the neglected ledger. With a sigh, she pulled it toward her. There was no way she could go anywhere, at least not for the next six weeks. She had work to do!

Shortly before noon, Leigh called her friend Gail. Particularly now, with Gail in the late stages of pregnancy, she was careful not to interrupt her afternoon rest period. Many women had trouble carrying multiple babies full term, but for a diabetic the problem was definitely compounded. Gail needed to conserve her strength and she tried conscientiously to do so. Each day that she could keep from delivering prematurely meant that the babies had that much more time to get a good lease on life.

Leigh made her voice as cheerful as possible: "How are things at the Martindale house?"

"Pretty good." Gail didn't sound very perky. Leigh knew that the hot weather was hard on her, as were all those extra inches around her midsection. "I've forgotten what my toes look like, but I suspect they're fat too."

Leigh couldn't help laughing. "Listen," she suggested, "why don't you plan on spending tomorrow with me? It's much cooler out here than in town. What say I come pick you up first thing in the morning? I'll plan a light fruit salad for lunch, and then we can spend the afternoon in a shady, walled garden beside a beautiful turquoise pool. Maybe swim a few lazy laps. Kit is welcome to come join us after work. We'll barbecue hamburgers for dinner."

"What a heavenly suggestion. Are you sure I wouldn't be keeping you from anything important?"

"No. Actually, I'm overdue for a day off. You'll be doing me a favor. What do you say?"

Gail laughed. "I say yes, yes, yes!"

The day proved to be every bit as relaxing as they had both hoped. Leigh warned her friend in advance about Tumbleweed's idiosyncrasies. The massive dog was delighted to greet another woman who had, in his opinion, the good sense to avoid the use of smelly perfumes. But Leigh was nervous about the possibility of the shaggy, big mutt leaping up in his usual exuberant way and perhaps causing Gail to lose her balance and fall. She soon ushered the dog out into his own part of the yard. That attended to, the two women strolled through the colorful flower garden, then settled down near the pool for a long visit.

"I gather that Kit and the fellow who owns this house nearly came to blows the first night they met." Gail's eyes twinkled merrily as she coaxed Leigh into telling her all the details. "Did you really think he was a burglar?"

"Yes, I'm afraid I did. And he was pretty suspicious of me too. Imagine arriving home after a long, hard trip to be zapped by an airborne Mickey Finn — and then find that the stranger occupying your house was all set to have the police arrest you!"

Leigh added that once the misunderstandings had been straightened out, the two men had gotten along just fine. She didn't expand on the reasons why she was still house-sitting the Wainwright home. It would have seemed like a betrayal of confidence to tell anyone, even someone as discreet as Gail, about the baffling way that Carlos's discoveries were being pirated away before he could claim them. She merely remarked that the petrogeologist had plans to be in and out a good bit during the next week or two, and he preferred not to leave his beautiful home unattended.

"But he's solved the problem of preserving my good reputation in a most unique way. Wait until you meet my chaperones!"

The nuns took their meals at the convent in town. As usual, though, they arrived back early. After greeting Leigh's friends and making their usual fuss over Tumbleweed, they took themselves off to their own quarters and their review of the day's language studies.

"That's what I call ingenuity," Kit said. "This arrangement stops the gossips cold, and performs a good deed at the same time."

Leigh had had an unusually lazy day. Now she insisted on turning her comfortable chaise lounge over to Kit while she got out the meat and flamed up the barbecue. On the way back from town that morning, she and Gail had stopped at a roadside produce stand where she'd purchased plump, golden ears of corn, vine-fresh salad vegetables, and the fruit they'd had for lunch. She buttered the ears of corn, then wrapped them in foil. Once the mesquite-flavored charcoal blazed and subsided into glowing embers, the corn was positioned on the grate to roast slowly.

Leigh sliced tomatoes, onions, and dill pickles. Crisp lettuce leaves were washed and drained. As she flipped the sizzling meat on the grill with a spatula, she noticed that Kit had pushed his own chaise right up alongside Gail's. The young husband and wife were holding hands while having a quiet tête-à-tête over the day's events.

It didn't look exciting, but that was what she, too, wanted out of life, Leigh decided wistfully. Someone who'd stay in love with her even when she was wearing maternity clothes. A husband who'd be eager to share his victories and disappointments, and be ready to listen understandingly to hers.

A sudden burst of giggles punctuated the conversation on the other side of the pool. *That too,* she thought. It was important to be able to laugh even if things didn't always turn out the way you'd planned.

She wished she knew if Carlos Wainwright would match this image of her dream man.

On his last evening in Oklahoma City, Carlos phoned home to let Leigh know he'd be arriving early the next day. "Tell Sentry to expect me," he warned.

"I will." Leigh repressed a chuckle. It would probably be years before Carlos saw anything funny about his first meeting with the security system.

After answering his queries about Tumbleweed and the nuns, she told him that she had interviewed and hired two new house-sitters that day. "They seem to be very efficient," she added. "Maybe one of them could take over here for me."

"What a terrible idea!" A stunned silence followed this outburst. "I mean — well, after all," Carlos added hastily, "you know where everything is. And Tumbleweed loves you. Don't you like it there anymore?"

More than anyplace else in the world, Leigh thought.

"Sure I do," she said aloud, more pleased than she'd have thought possible at his vehement reaction. "But that was just a short-term contract I signed with Brenda. It'll be coming to an end soon."

"Yeah." Carlos didn't sound particularly enthusiastic about the prospect. "And I still haven't a clue as to who's been pulling a fast one on me. You haven't had any attempts at break-ins there, have you?"

"No, thank goodness!"

From what he had told her before, Leigh could think of no possible way the thefts could be taking place from the house. In fact, unless there was a larcenous mind reader out there somewhere, there didn't seem to be *any* way for the well-guarded secrets to be finding their way into the wrong hands.

She passed on the message from his sister, but skipped going into details about the conversation she'd overheard between Serita and her fiancé. "Were you planning on doing any free-lance oil prospecting on your way to and from Texas?" she asked.

"I don't know." Carlos sounded discouraged. "There's a very promising area not far off the route, and I've been wanting to investigate it thoroughly. But the way things have been going the past few months, I'm almost hoping *not* to find anything good."

Leigh understood. While the challenge of making the discovery appealed to Carlos, he hated the possibility that his pioneering might lead to a bonanza for the thieves.

"Too bad there isn't some way to delude them," she said. "Do a bit of sleight of hand to make them believe you've found something really stupendous. Let them go to a whole lot of trouble to get it for themselves, only to find —"

"That there's nothing there except sagebrush and a nest of diamondback rattlers!" Carlos was definitely thinking along the same lines as she. "Yes, that would suit me fine. If I can think up a convincing feint, I'll let you know."

She heard a yawn being muffled on the other end of the line. It had taken several days of nonstop work to wind up the contract job for the oil company, she knew. "Meanwhile," she said, "it sounds like you need a few solid hours of sleep so you'll be clear-headed for tomorrow's flight. Good night, Carlos."

For the next hour or so, Leigh continued to mull over the possibility of tricking the crooks into snapping at the wrong bait. Unfortunately, she couldn't figure out a way to make that happen. If only they knew *how* the information was vanishing! With that lead to follow, they might be able to set a trap and nab the crooks. Right now, Carlos was doing battle with the great unknown, which certainly gave him a handicap. You couldn't

110

hoax what you couldn't see.

It was only later, after she had bathed and crawled into bed, that Leigh realized she hadn't asked how the plane was behaving. Carlos hadn't mentioned having any engine trouble on the trip east. On the day he had worked on the oil-pressure gauge, he'd convinced her that he was extremely safety-minded. She felt sure he wouldn't risk flying if there was even one questionable piece of machinery in his plane. Nevertheless, she wished she had brought up the subject. Being assured that everything was okay would have set her mind at ease. And she would have let him know that her thoughts were with him.

She rolled over, pounding her pillow, willing sleep to come. He'd get home safely. Of course he would!

As usual, the next morning Leigh started work before eight o'clock. She had trouble settling down to any one task, though. During the next two hours she accomplished very little business. She gave up pretending at last, relinked her phone to the answering machine, and whistled for Tumbleweed. Together they headed across the open countryside on foot.

Some of her anxiety seemed to communicate itself to the dog. He'd chase off, then run back yapping. On one return trip he deposited an ancient bone at her feet. The next time he chased a rabbit her way, as if inviting her to join in the hunt. Leigh tossed a stick for him, an apology for being such poor company.

Watching the arc of wood soaring through the clear, bright air, she caught a flash of silver on the distant horizon. As it droned closer she made out the outline of a small, familiar aircraft. A spurt of exhilaration charged through her veins. Spinning around, she headed for the runway.

Twenty yards away, the plane touched down and streaked past. She caught sight of Carlos bent over the controls. By the time he had swung into a turn at the far end of the runway and taxied slowly back, she was waiting at the edge of the tarmac. An excited, quivering beast danced from paw to paw at her side.

"A welcoming committee! How great!"

As Carlos climbed out of the cockpit, his face lit up with pleasure at the sight of the team who had come to meet him. He tucked his gloves into a pocket of the leather jacket and reached forward to reward Tumbleweed with a pat on the head. Then he straightened up and gazed into Leigh's shining eyes.

"I always like to save the best for last," he said. "What are you doing out here?"

"Oh, I —" Leigh's heart was pounding like a brass drum. It was a wonder he couldn't hear it. "I needed a little fresh air. Imagine my astonishment when a plane suddenly landed, right here in the backyard."

"Yes, such a surprise!" He held out his arms and hugged her close. "What a little coward you are, Leigh, afraid to even own up that you're glad to see me. Why don't you just say 'welcome home'? That way, you wouldn't be committing yourself to anything."

"Welcome home, Carlos. It's so good to see you."

Leigh closed her eyes and raised her lips for his kiss. The pressure of his mouth on hers was wonderfully warm and caring. Holding him tight, she marveled at his insight. How could he have known about her confusion? She wished she dared love him without reservations, but was terrified of bestowing her heart for fear he might someday reject it.

She was trembling when at last she moved back from his embrace.

Carlos trailed his fingers through her curls, then looped a sturdy arm across her shoulders. "If you don't stop shaking, I'll begin to feel like the big, bad wolf. What's the matter, Leigh?"

She took a deep breath, pulling herself together. "It's so silly. You'll probably think I'm a nut. But when we talked on the phone last night, I forgot to ask how the plane was running. I started worrying about something going wrong, and got more and more agitated."

"I had an inkling that might be the trouble." Curling a hand around each arm, Carlos drew her toward him, all the while gazing deeply into her eyes. "My plane is a well-maintained piece of machinery. More than that, I'm a very good pilot. You are never, never to worry about me in the air again. Do you promise? If I can't depend on you to do this, I'll have to get a new profession. That would be a shame. I happen to be very fond of the way I make my living."

Like his words, his face was extraordinarily intent. There was no doubt at all that he meant every syllable. Leigh paled and caught her breath.

"You'd get a new job on account of *me?*"

He nodded somberly. "There wouldn't be any choice. I've read about wives of auto racers and highway patrolmen dying a thousand deaths every time their husband walks out of the house, because they're so terrified something might happen to him. That's not going to be the case with you and me. I love you and I'm pretty darned sure you love me too. You'll get around to admitting it one of these days when you quit fretting about all the differences in our backgrounds and let yourself see that, in the ways that count, we're very much alike. But I meant what I said. I won't turn the girl I adore into a basket case. I'd sell the plane and learn to be a — landscape gardener."

She wanted to laugh and cry at the same time. Emotions crowded in on her. "A landscape gardener!" she repeated tremulously. "Oh, Carlos, don't do that. Poor Tumbleweed would never survive if you came home from work every day reeking of flowers!"

"It's up to you. Give me your word."

Leigh reached out to circle his waist. "Carlos, I love you so. And you were right. All the way down the line. It *has* worried me because we've seemed to have so little in common. Yet you're the one man in the world I want to go through life with. Even if we share just one thing — the fact that we love each other — I'm convinced it will be enough."

He sighed in relief and hugged her close. Then, once more, he drew back. "What about the rest of it?"

"I promise not to drive myself crazy worrying about you. Whenever you leave me behind on the ground, I'll keep the faith that you'll come back safely, that nothing bad will happen, and that we'll soon be together again. There! You have my solemn word on it."

Strong hands framed her face. Carlos bent forward and kissed her with all the sweet, yearning love at his command. "I'll keep the faith too. Wherever I go, I'll take you with me in my heart. Will you marry me, Leigh?"

She took a trembly breath. Could he really take a chance on a girl like her? Someone whose own parents had walked away from her?

"Did — did you say you wanted to marry me?"

"For ever and ever. The love I have for you is going to make up for everything else you missed out on over the years."

The tears in her eyes spilled over. He always seemed to know exactly what she was thinking. Heart and soul, they matched.

"I didn't know it was possible to be this happy," she whispered. "Yes, Carlos, yes. I'll marry you!"

When it came to getting any work accomplished, the afternoon turned out to be even less productive than the morning had been. With Leigh snuggled close by, Carlos placed long-distance calls to his parents in Australia and his older sister in Alaska. Jubilantly, he announced that he had found the perfect girl. He and his bride-to-be wanted to be married as soon as possible. Would the family be able to attend? When would it be possible for them to come, so that a date for the ceremony could be set?

Leigh gathered that a major undertaking such as this was going to require a good bit of coordination and advance planning. Ines, his sister, whooped with joy. She promised to start working on getting a leave of absence for her husband that very day.

Mrs. Wainwright didn't mention the vast distances involved. She made it very clear that they wouldn't dream of missing their son's wedding. Her husband was away in the Outback. Within the next few days, however, Samuel was due to arrive in Tennant Creek to replenish his supplies. He always contacted her the moment he came to a locality with a phone. She promised to find out how soon he could put his work on hold in order to make the trip. Within a week, they'd have some definite word to pass on.

When he had hung up the second time, Leigh asked where his mother lived while his father went off to the back of beyond.

"In Alice Springs," Carlos replied. "That's

a small but important town near the center of Australia. It lies three or four hundred miles south of Tennant Creek in an enormous state called the Northern Territories. In some ways, it's rather like New Mexico. Hot and dry in most seasons. Mother works with both children and adults, teaching them to play various musical instruments. She is especially skilled at using music as therapy for people with learning disabilities."

Leigh began to realize that she'd had the wrong idea about the delicate-looking woman whose ancestors had come from Spain so many centuries ago. They might have been aristocrats, but they were also doers.

"Then your father goes out to these empty parts of the Outback to look for water?"

Carlos explained that the vast center of the Land Down Under was mostly desert and grazing lands for the huge sheep stations. "The stations are what we would call ranches here. Believe it or not, some of them cover areas of several thousand square miles. It's terribly dry there most of the time. That's why my father's ability to find water almost by instinct and advise people where to sink their wells is so valuable. Water makes the difference between life and death."

"Doesn't your mother miss him? Worry

about him while he's gone?"

"Of course she does," Carlos said. "Because they each have work to do that they consider very important, they're separated quite a lot of the time. Ah, but their reunions are something else!"

That was the way it would be with them, Leigh thought. Though their separations wouldn't be so long and drawn out, she and Carlos would often be apart in the future because of the nature of their work. But whenever he came home, how they would appreciate the chance to be together!

Later that day they drove into Santa Fe. They strolled from shop to shop until they found exactly the right stone for Leigh's engagement ring. The beautiful, square-cut aquamarine was the same lively shade as her eyes. While at the jeweler's, they also chose a set of matching wedding rings.

Then, knowing it was now late enough for Kit to be home from work, they paid a surprise call on the Martindales to announce their happy news. Carlos and Leigh invited the other couple to join them for dinner.

Unfortunately, Gail's strength was not up to a night out, but she promised that they would hold a real celebration after the babies arrived.

"While you were gone, she came out and

spent a whole day with me," Leigh told Carlos as they walked back out to his car. "Just being around the pool helped. This hot weather is terribly hard for her to cope with."

Carlos said that as far as he was concerned, Leigh's friend was welcome to spend all the time she wanted at his swimming pool. "Did she use the word 'babies'?" he asked.

"Yes, the doctor can hear two heartbeats distinctly, but he says that he can't be certain whether there's a third. Kit and Gail may wind up the parents of triplets."

Gail's due date was toward the end of September, so she had nearly two months yet to go. Gail hoped to last out the full term since multiple babies tended to be underweight. She had to be extremely careful with her diet. So far, she'd managed to keep her diabetes under control without medication. She didn't want to have to start taking insulin.

Carlos left a note for the nuns, asking that they please give Tumbleweed his supper. The sisters had become old hands at coping with Sentry by now. The newly engaged couple felt free to go out to dinner to celebrate the happy occasion.

"How about eating at The Katcina Doll?" he suggested.

Leigh agreed enthusiastically. She had

been in the restaurant only once before. Its decor was most unusual, focusing on the Katcina dolls that were a traditional part of Hopi Indian life. The wooden figurines were carved and decorated to represent super-natural beings. Hopi children learned about the ancient spirits of their tribe through the dolls and the designs on their clothing.

After they had selected their dinner from the ethnic menu, Carlos told Leigh that a few summers earlier he had visited Hopiland in Arizona during the tribe's exciting August festivals. The highlight of his visit was watching the men, dressed in Katcina costumes, performing the ceremonial Snake dances.

Previously, Carlos had been unable to contact Serita. The following morning, though, she answered her phone. He wasted no time in telling her the good news about his impending marriage.

"Congratulations, big brother! That makes two of us Wainwrights headed for the altar," Serita exclaimed. She seemed aware of the deep mistrust with which Carlos viewed her future husband. "You haven't changed your mind about that trip to Dallas you promised to take, have you?"

"No, I thought I would fly down for a day or two at the end of the week." He said nothing about hoping to persuade her to postpone her own marriage, at least until their parents could return home and check out her fiancé for themselves.

"I've been hoping you'll decide to let me draw on part of my inheritance ahead of time," Serita said. "Denny says it's important to put the new pump into service as soon as we possibly can. And what's a few months, after all?"

"Sorry, Sis. I didn't write that will. Grandfather did. I'm just your guardian while the folks are out of the country. Ines and I had to wait until we came of age, and I'm afraid you'll have to do the same."

Hearing her brother's firm tone, Serita abandoned her coaxing efforts and asked for all the rest of the family news.

Hearing them talk about finances gave Leigh an uneasy sensation. It seemed obvious to her that Serita was being subjected to more than a little pressure by her eager fiancé. Legally, of course, there was nothing Denny Cahill could do. Until Serita turned twenty-one, the money was safely tied up.

Somehow, though, Leigh had a feeling that he hadn't given up trying to have things his own way.

Chapter Seven

Four days later, a call was put through to Santa Fe from the other side of the world, and the next thing she knew, Leigh was receiving an earful of warm good wishes from her future father-in-law. Judging from the hearty congratulations he next bestowed on his son, Samuel Wainwright was thoroughly in favor of the upcoming marriage.

"Always did trust your good judgment, my boy," he said. "I know the girl you've chosen must be lovely in every way. Sorry to say, though, it's likely to be almost eight weeks before I can take any time off. These wells are all at a crucial stage of drilling. But after that, your mother and I will be able to stay in the States for a couple of months, and get in a nice, long visit with all our family and friends. Would you be willing to postpone the wedding until the first week in October?"

Carlos pretended to hesitate, then laughed. "If I had my way, Dad, I'd marry her tomorrow. Guess I'd better learn to practice patience. To tell the truth, Leigh's best friend is expecting a baby very shortly, and

I think it would please her to wait a few weeks until Gail can be matron of honor at the ceremony."

Touched by his thoughtfulness, Leigh nodded in agreement. "Yes, I'd love that. October sounds perfect. Oh, and tell your father it won't be a big, fancy wedding. Just a very special day for us and our families."

Carlos finished the long-distance conversation with a lump in his throat. Families. He could still remember the sharp, quick stab of jealousy he'd felt the first time he heard Kit Martindale call Leigh "sweetheart." Soon afterward he realized he'd misunderstood their relationship entirely. Nowadays, he and the young inventor regarded each other with mutual respect. But he knew that, to Leigh, Kit and Gail were far more than friends. In her view they were family — all the family she had.

This reflection reminded him of an idea that had struck him during the flight home from Oklahoma City. It was a long shot, of course. Still, you never knew. Something might come of it. He wanted to try, anyway.

Since there was no time like the present, he stood up and fished in his pocket for the car keys. Leigh looked rather surprised. "Going into town?" she asked.

"Yes." Carlos tried to act nonchalant, and

hoped she wouldn't suggest going along. "Thought I might stop by the convent for a few minutes. It's been ages since I've seen my Aunt Carmelita. I'll introduce the two of you sometime soon, when she isn't so busy."

"Sure. Come to think of it, I promised to call the plumbers about the work they did at the Stuart house. Angelina claims that the drains are still clogged partially. Oh, and she wants me to call the vet too. She says she's been finding feathers all over the house. It sounds like their darned parakeet is starting to molt."

"Either that or the itchy cat has been nibbling."

Carlos covered his relief with a laugh. Angelina's problems with her summer house-sitting job were becoming legendary. He seriously doubted whether Sitting Tight would ever be willing to contract with the Stuart family for a repeat assignment.

"Go ahead and tend to business, by all means." He gave her an affectionate kiss, then drew back with a sigh. Eight weeks, at least, until they'd be husband and wife. "See you later."

Leigh heard the garage door swing shut. The Trans-Am reversed down the driveway and turned off in the direction of Santa Fe. It sounded, she thought with satisfaction, as if he was holding the speed under the limit. Good!

Then a little frown worked its way in between her brows. It seemed like a peculiar time for him to be visiting his aunt, especially after his remark about how busy she was. But maybe he had a message to pass on to her from his parents.

That evening the engaged couple sat down with a calendar and a notepad. They chose October tenth as their wedding date. Then they began listing all the things that needed to be taken care of well ahead of time. It was appalling, the number of complicated arrangements that even a small ceremony seemed to require.

"First thing we'd better do is decide on how many people we want to ask, so that the printer can start working on the invitations," Carlos suggested. "And speaking of immediate problems, I guess I ought to get that trip to Dallas out of the way. I wish I could think of some way to make my sister see reason about this character she's so determined to marry. Anyhow, I'm going to insist she hold off doing anything drastic until our folks arrive."

"She's really looking forward to seeing you again," Leigh reminded him. She knew how relieved Carlos would be to hand the responsibility for his younger sister back to his parents. But she could see Serita's point also. Everyone wanted to be independent. "Just try not to sound too bossy. Good advice isn't all that easy to swallow, you know, even when it comes from a fond big brother."

"Want to come along and referee?"

"No, thank you!" Leigh said. "I have no intention of starting off on the wrong foot with my future sister-in-law. Just make sure you count to ten if you get the urge to punch Denny Cahill. And call me at least once a day, will you?"

"You can come along even if you don't actually climb into the ring with us," Carlos coaxed. He cuddled her in a warm embrace.

Leigh shook her head. "It isn't that I don't want to go with you. I'd love to sit in that right-hand seat and watch you handle the controls. But I haven't made any advance arrangements for someone to take over Sitting Tight. Next time we'll plan ahead."

"Darned right."

Looking as if there were plenty of things he'd rather be doing, Carlos headed out across the field to take care of a comprehensive preflight check of his plane before the next morning's takeoff. If he had the chance while in Dallas, he remarked upon his return to the house, he would have a regular aviation mechanic do a thorough tune-up of the engine. But he was determined to make this a quick trip. He'd try to talk some sense into Serita, then get home to Santa Fe as soon as possible.

"No detours?" Leigh asked. "You mentioned something about exploring an area you considered a potential oil field."

Carlos jammed his hands into his pockets. "I'm going to keep that one under my hat for the time being. I don't want to risk giving those pirates a crack at anything else I discover."

Leigh felt a pang upon watching his plane lift off early the next morning. Then she reminded herself that there would be many such partings in the years ahead. During the course of their marriage, she and Carlos would be separating briefly a great many times. She forced a grin as she walked back to the house. It was those reunions she intended to look forward to!

She still hadn't quite mastered the knack of not worrying, though. Leigh felt a guilty stab of relief when Carlos rang her from Dallas a few hours later to report his safe arrival.

"Serita is on her way to pick me up," he added, sounding resigned. "Cahill is coming with her, worse luck. Wouldn't you think that guy had other things to do than tag along?"

"Well, it *is* Saturday," Leigh reminded him. "Only workaholics like us who run our own businesses have to work weekends. Maybe you two will hit it off better this time."

"We're likely to hit it off, all right."

The grumble sounded pretty negative. Hoping he'd find a way to smile when greeting Denny Cahill, Leigh asked whether Carlos had arranged with a mechanic to do the plane's tune-up.

"No. As you pointed out, it's Saturday. All the weekend fliers are here, tinkering and claiming the attention of the few mechanics on duty. I'll have everything taken care of in Santa Fe. The grease monkeys at the airport there know the plane inside out, anyway. I'd rather trust them —" The blare of a horn interrupted. "Here's Serita," he said quickly, and threw her a kiss over the miles. "Talk to you later."

Early that evening Leigh spent a half hour visiting with the nuns. Their stay in the house was nearing its end. Within another week, Sister Bernadette said, their courses in the Indian dialects would be over. Then the large group of teachers would disperse to the four corners of the state again. Some would be returning to city schools where they taught year after year. Others would be assigned to various mission schools. Often, these were located on the Indian reservations.

"We just go where we're needed," she said, smiling. "The children are so anxious to learn. Teaching in even the most rural areas is a pleasure."

"This is the last trip Carlos will be making for a while," Leigh said. "As soon as he returns from Texas, I'll be moving back into town until after our wedding in October. It's certainly been a pleasure to share the house with you all."

"And we've appreciated your hospitality." Sister Bernadette gave Tumbleweed a pat on his shaggy head, then brushed some sandy hair from her habit. "It's hard to decide which of your watchdogs we'll miss the most, this fellow or Sentry. I'm just sorry we never had the opportunity to see the security system in action."

"I'm not!" Leigh laughed. "Sentry is really awesome. Knowing your kind heart, you'd probably wind up feeling sorry for the burglar." She detailed her lone experience in that line. "That's what happened to me, and now I'm engaged to marry the guy!"

After bidding them good night, Leigh returned down the hall. She was just passing her office room when the phone began to ring. Though she often kept it hooked up to the answering machine, she had not done so tonight because of Carlos's promise to call her later. Now she ran to her desk and snatched up the receiver.

"Hello! Is that you, Leigh?"

Swallowing her disappointment, she dropped into her chair. The voice on the other end of the line belonged not to the man she loved but to Roger MacKenzie.

"You have your phone service hooked up at the Seven Cities of Cibola already, I see. That's really fast work."

"It isn't like you to be snide, Leigh."

His reproving tone made her laugh. "No, I guess it isn't. I'm sorry. What's the trouble?"

"You hit the nail right on the head — trouble! I need a huge favor. My van has a broken axle."

Having embarked on his tale of woe, Roger continued to pour out the details. He still maintained that the clues unearthed from his research materials were perfectly valid. Unfortunately, there wasn't so much as a mule trail that led within miles of where he believed the Seven Cities of Cibola would be found. The terrain in the backcountry was too rugged for even his sturdy four-wheel-drive vehicle to handle.

"I left my van and managed to hitchhike back to a crossroads trading post. But the tow truck operator refuses to budge unless someone guarantees payment in advance."

"Can't you do that yourself?"

"Oh, come on, Leigh! I had a few bucks in my jeans for gas and a bit extra to spend on food. A man has to eat, after all. But I sure wasn't prepared for a costly emergency."

"You wouldn't be, not with those rose-colored glasses you always wear," she muttered under her breath. But aloud she murmured a few soothing words about hard luck.

"I knew you'd understand," Roger cut in gratefully. "Could you run into town and hand the people at his main office one of your company checks? That's the only way he'll agree to haul my van out of that chuckhole it's in. You wouldn't mind doing that for a faithful employee, would you?"

"What was that about a *faithful* employee?"

He chuckled at the reminder of how he'd left her in the lurch. "Oh, yeah. I'm really sorry about that, Leigh. Believe me, it'll never happen again. And listen, if you'll bail me out this once, I'll house-sit off the towing fee without a single word of complaint. Even if it takes until Thanksgiving. But you'll have to hurry. That bandit out there wants cash on the barrel, and he claims his dispatcher goes home at seven."

Had it not been for Roger's sticking her with this job, she would never have met Carlos, Leigh reminded herself. Besides, the poor guy was desperate. And when he tended to business instead of running off to pursue a legend, he really was an excellent house-sitter. She could always make use of his services.

"Okay, I'll do it," she agreed. "Hope everything goes all right with your van. Check with me in a day or two. I'll see about finding you a new assignment."

She cut short his thanks and hurried out to her car, intent on completing the errand and making it back again before Carlos called. Roger could really be a pain in the neck. But who knew? Maybe that head-in-the-clouds historian really was destined to make a great discovery someday. If so, it surely would be fun to point out his name in the history books to her grandchildren!

"How is everyone getting along?"

It was late the following day. By now, Leigh thought, her fiancé had been in Dallas long enough to make friends with a whole nighttime soap opera full of unpleasant characters. She hoped he was doing well with the two people he'd flown down to visit.

That thought was far too optimistic. Angrily, Carlos reported that Denny Cahill had kept putting forward logical-sounding explanations why Serita should have her inheritance a few months early. "He says that by her birthday, the cold weather will be practically upon them. He claims that that will make it far more difficult to demonstrate the capabilities of the new pump to the oilmen who constitute his potential market."

"Hmm," Leigh said dubiously. "Texas is sitting way down there in the Sun Belt. I'm sure they do get *some* winter, but —"

"Exactly," Carlos took her point grouchily. "But to hear him talk, you'd think that everything north of Corpus Christi turned to Arctic tundra come Halloween. Serita seems to be trapped in the middle of the dispute. I can tell she truly doesn't care about the money. It's just that, being engaged to him, she feels she ought to side with Cahill."

Torn loyalties could certainly make things difficult, Leigh agreed. She decided that occasionally there might be a tiny silver lining to having no family at all. At least she never had problems like this to cope with.

"What are you going to do?" she asked.

"I'm going to get in my airplane tomorrow

morning and come home." From his satisfied tone of voice, the prospect seemed to appeal to Carlos. "I'll have breakfast with Serita, and suggest that she throw her problems in our parents' laps. After that, I'll be on my way. With any sort of a tailwind, I ought to be home by two at the latest."

"Speaking of wind, it's really beginning to kick up a fuss out here," Leigh said apprehensively. She walked over to the window and peered out at the gathering gloom. Even in the sheltered courtyard, trees were thrashing back and forth. Beyond the thick adobe wall she caught a glimpse of dust devils twirling menacingly around in the sandy stretches of the open countryside.

"It's beautiful and clear here," Carlos said, but he agreed that New Mexico's sudden summer storms could be nasty. Solemnly, he promised to check the weather forecast before taking off the following morning. If the route to the northwest looked too ominous, he would delay his departure and advise her immediately of the change of plan.

"Good." His calm, sensible attitude made Leigh feel better. She was eager to see him again, but not at the risk of his safety. "I love you, Carlos."

"Love you too. See you tomorrow."

By bedtime the storm had begun in earnest. Leigh snapped the leash onto Tumble-weed's collar when they braved the wind to take their last ramble of the day. Bundled up in a heavy sweater and scarf, she allowed him to go no farther than absolutely necessary. For once, he didn't seem inclined to dally. She wondered if he remembered the terrible storm that had separated him from his mother when he was just a small puppy, leaving him tangled in that thorny desert bush until Carlos came to his rescue.

Several times during the night Leigh awoke when an exceptionally forceful gust of wind struck the house. Even the thick adobe walls seemed to shudder from the impact. With a concerned glance at the device on her nightstand, she thought how fortunate it was that Sentry wasn't motion-sensitive. There'd be alarms ringing frantically all over town if that were the case.

The awareness of the many houses her little company was responsible for kept her from dozing back off after that. Even though her employees were capable and trustworthy people, she couldn't help feeling a twinge of anxiety.

Finally, at a little before five A.M., Tumbleweed's whines from the kitchen gave her an excuse to get up. She climbed out of bed, shivering at the chill in her dark room, and pulled on the thickest clothing she had brought out from her apartment in town.

After comforting the nervous dog, she gave him something to eat, then put a pot of coffee on to perk. Half an hour later, the nuns hurried down the hall with rain slickers over their arms and warm black shawls wrapped around their summerweight habits.

Sister Bernadette paused with Leigh near the door, and they frowned up at the sky. Daylight seemed to be fighting a losing battle with the ugly thunderheads rolling in from the north.

"This is the first time since we arrived that I wish our lodgings were closer to the Mission," the nun said.

Obviously, she wasn't looking forward to the usually restful drive into Santa Fe. Especially at the end of a hot, dry summer, when the ground had been baked into a brick of unyielding clay, flash floods were a real danger.

"Watch out if it starts to rain," Leigh warned. "We've been known to get some ferocious gully-washers around here."

Alone in the house now, she carefully checked each window, making sure none had been left open for dampness to seep through. Next, she brought in a heap of wood and stacked it in readiness beside the fireplace.

Lightning splintered the sky, followed by an explosion of thunder not a heartbeat behind. *Close,* she thought, shuddering. Seconds later, a torrential downpour began. Rain pelted out of the sky with such violent force that it seemed as if a giant hand had suddenly yanked an opaque drapery across the outside of the window. Though Leigh had edgily been expecting it, the intensity of the deluge left her awed. And frightened. There had been just barely enough time for the nuns to get into town. Anyone else commuting this morning had better pull over.

Leigh swallowed hard. Why was she trying to kid herself? It wasn't the people out on the roads that her worried thoughts revolved around, though she certainly prayed the storm would cause no accidents. It was Carlos, who had planned to fly home from Dallas today, who gripped her thoughts.

Remembering the promises they had made to each other helped calm her fears. She had given her word not to let fear take a paralyzing grip on her heart while he was in the air. And only last night Carlos had assured her that he would pay careful attention to the meteorological report before attempting to take off.

He was a sharp, experienced pilot. He had logged hundreds of hours of flying time, over all sorts of terrain, under every weather condition imaginable. Leigh had utter faith in his ability and good sense. She knew that he would never risk his life or his aircraft by foolishly challenging an ominous weather front. He would either stay on the ground until it passed or rearrange his flight pattern so as to detour far around any turbulence.

Carlos, she assured herself once again, was all right. Texas was on Central Time, an hour ahead of Santa Fe. By now, he was undoubtedly sitting down to breakfast with Serita, making one last attempt to get her to see reason. After that, he would decide what to do about the trip home. If he thought it best to postpone the flight, she'd be the first to know.

Meanwhile, Leigh told herself, she had plenty of valid concerns if she was really determined to worry. Eighteen houses were under contract for Sitting Tight's guaranteed care. That was a heavy responsibility for one small business, and one she could not afford to neglect.

She poured herself a second cup of coffee. Carrying it to her desk, she dialed the first of the calls she made every morning to her employees. She gave thanks that for once Angelina had no new complaints about the Stuart family's blithe tendency to overlook normal maintenance on their home. Several of her other house-sitters, though, had encountered problems because of the storm. A downspout had clogged, causing a flood of water to funnel into somebody's basement. Several of her people reported that shingles and roof tiles had been ripped off during the night's high winds. In one area west of town, power lines were down.

While Leigh could do nothing to speed up restoration of the electricity, she made calming, practical suggestions to the sitters affected by the outage. Next, she put in calls to roofing, plumbing, and gardening firms kept on a retainer fee by Sitting Tight. The most urgent cases were given top priority. She was assured that all the problems would be taken care of within the next few hours.

Leigh slumped back in her chair, giving her aching throat a chance for a brief rest. She eyed her cold coffee distastefully. A brisk trip to the kitchen took care of two errands: letting Tumbleweed out for a quick run, and popping open a can of soda for herself. In her agitation over the storm she had skipped breakfast. Now she cut a slice of cheese from a wedge in the refrigerator, grabbed a handful of crackers and a bunch of grapes, and returned to her office.

During the entire morning she'd stayed

alert for incoming calls. More than ever now she was glad they'd had the telephone company install the second line, leaving one open at all times. That way Leigh could conduct her extremely phone-oriented business while leaving a number free for Carlos's call. She couldn't understand why he still hadn't phoned to let her know that his return to Santa Fe would be delayed by a day.

She tidied her papers, checked on the morning mail, and forced herself to eat a few more bites. Just before noon she dialed the Martindales.

"Kit is out in the kitchen, fixing me some chicken soup," Gail reported. "I was awake part of the night with back pains, and he decided to stay home from work today just in case a mad dash to the hospital should be called for. So far, so good, thank heavens."

"Enjoy the coddling while you can," Leigh advised. "One of these days you'll both be warming up bottles, and — Oh, darn!"

"What's the matter? Leigh!"

She hastened to reassure her friend: "Nothing unusual, all things considered. The lights just went off, that's all. I was expecting it. Some neighborhoods lost their power last night or early this morning. I'm glad there's a gas stove out here. I'll be able to fix a hot dinner even if they don't have the service restored right away. You guys had better get out the candles and flashlights too, just in case the same thing happens there."

Leigh groaned as she put down the phone and peered around the suddenly much dimmer room. Power outages could last for hours — days even, if the transformer had been struck by lightning and the utility company was really overburdened. While it was true that the kitchen stove didn't run on electricity, the pilot light for the central-heating unit did. She had a feeling that by evening she'd be glad she had taken the trouble to bring in all that wood for the fireplace.

As she unearthed candles, extra flashlights, and a lantern from the cupboard where emergency supplies were stored, Leigh finally admitted to herself that it wasn't just the power failure that was making her increasingly nervous. The fact that she hadn't heard from Carlos since the previous evening had her definitely on edge. He had promised to call immediately if there was to be any change in his plans. She should have heard from him hours ago!

To make sure the phone lines were still in service, she picked up the receiver of the nearest extension, held it to her ear, and pushed the appropriate buttons to test each line in turn. Both dial tones were humming away efficiently. Carlos could have gotten through anytime he'd called.

If he'd called. Obviously, he had not, which meant he was on his way.

Chewing her lip, she turned toward the window. Only a sporadic shower dashed against the glass now. The rain was rapidly moving southwest, propelled by the fierce, whistling winds that had been causing such havoc here. Oddly enough, the high desert landscape looked almost dry again. Ravines and arroyos would be filled with the racing, brownish water that had cascaded out of the sky, across the land, and into ditches and low spots. But the cactus and sagebrush-strewn countryside surrounding the house looked as hard-packed as ever thanks to the force of the rains. None of the life-giving water had had a chance to sink in.

More than that, though, she noticed in relief that the sky definitely seemed to be clearing. That must be the explanation, Leigh decided. Weather forecasts available to aviators were highly accurate and timely. Carlos would have been informed not only about the storm by his meteorological source, but also of the clearing pattern to follow. He'd been truly eager to get away from Dallas. If the forecast had indicated that by the time he was ready to land, Santa

Fe would be under clear skies, he'd have taken off.

She looked longingly at the telephone. There were a couple of ways she could find out for sure. Calling Serita was one method. But she didn't want to upset Serita, to give her the idea that something might be wrong when, of course, it wasn't.

Or she could phone the airfield at Dallas. But that was a huge, busy place teaming with all types of aircraft. Trying to find the exact person who'd be able to tell her whether one small private plane had taken off that morning could be a frustrating, time-consuming job.

More than that, if word got back to Carlos that she'd called to check — and she knew it would — he might think that she hadn't had enough faith in him.

No, Leigh told herself. It was better to cross her fingers.

And wait.

Chapter Eight

At eight o'clock that evening she was still waiting. Though the rain was long gone, clouds still brooded along the edges of the sky, shadowing the dwindling rays of twilight. In another hour it would be dark. Really dark. Very few stars could pierce that gloomy overcast and make themselves seen by someone relying on them for accurate directions. Celestial navigation would be impossible.

With a terrible effort, Leigh made herself turn away from the window. She tried not to dwell on the scary realization that without those stars, Carlos had one-third less chance of making it home safely. He'd be relying fully on dead reckoning and his plane's inertial guidance system. And he himself had termed dead reckoning "educated guesswork." Educated or not, the notion that his life might depend on a hunch gave her a shaky, jelly-like feeling inside.

His instruments were accurate, she told herself. There was a compass and — and all those things. Pilots made landings on instruments alone all the time in the movies.

Sure, a niggling voice inside her head retorted, but that was with someone in a control tower on a regular field to talk the pilot down, to tell him exactly what to do and at what precise second to do it. Carlos wouldn't have that competent air-traffic controller here, or a commercial field. Or even the runway lights. His remote-control gadget wouldn't work, not tonight. All the power was still out.

He wouldn't know about that, she thought, trying very hard not to cry. He might get all the way here but then be forced to fly around and around and around, peering down for some familiar landmark. Searching. Thinking he might have underestimated the distance, and maybe heading farther north. And there were mountains. . . .

Reluctant as she was to let Carlos know she'd been doing anything as ridiculous as worrying about him, Leigh had thrown in the towel at six o'clock and placed a call to Texas. She had waited as long as sanity would allow. Even then he was four hours overdue.

Serita was at home. Yes, of course Carlos had taken off, she told Leigh. She had driven him out to the airport herself, then waited until his plane had disappeared into the distance.

"But that was at nine o'clock this morning," Serita said, her voice quavering. "Surely he must have shown up by now."

"No. No, he hasn't." Leigh hoped she didn't sound that shaky herself. "Last night he said he expected to be home by two at the latest. But since then we've had a terrible storm. I was hoping that he might have delayed his departure until tomorrow morning because of the weather."

"I don't believe he felt that was necessary," Serita said. "I know he checked with the airport the very last thing before leaving my apartment after breakfast. They told him the storm was already starting to blow clear of your area."

Leigh's heart sank. He had come ahead, then. Just as she'd assumed, he had radioed for an up-to-the-minute forecast and headed home. But where was he?

"It's less than six hundred miles from Dallas to Santa Fe," Serita said. "The flight shouldn't have taken nearly this long. Something dreadful must have happened!"

Willing away hysterics, Leigh sucked in a deep breath. It sure wouldn't help Carlos if she screeched with horror and passed out cold. No way. She and his sister had to stay calm. His life might depend on their fast, levelheaded action.

"Serita, it's obvious that something *did* happen, but hopefully it isn't anything more than a spot of engine trouble. If that was the case, he'd have put down on the first level stretch of pasture he caught sight of. You know how big those Texas spreads are. Chances are he's still hiking toward the ranch house."

"Sure, I should have figured that out for myself. That's exactly the sort of thing my brother would do." Serita's voice rang with forced bravado. "I'd better hang up now and phone the airport. Somebody there will know exactly how to activate a search party. Carlos would have logged a flight plan. It will be on record. The air patrol can just follow the same compass heading."

Until it's too dark to see anything, and they're forced to come home, Leigh thought. But tomorrow was another day, as good old Scarlett O'Hara always maintained. At first light the searchers would take wing again. Then they *would* find him. Safe!

That had been two hours and six pep talks ago. Serita had called back to let Leigh know that a search was getting underway. Since then, there had been nothing either of them could do except wait, hope

148

for the best, and pray.

Tumbleweed's dinner was long overdue. Leigh forced herself to walk briskly out to the kitchen. She opened a can of his favorite food and gave his shaggy head a few encouraging pats as she bent down to set the meaty dish in front of him. But tonight, the big dog seemed to sense that something was very wrong. Usually prone to gulp down every morsel, lick the plate, and look around for dessert, Tumbleweed left several succulent bites untasted tonight.

Leigh didn't blame him. She couldn't have swallowed a crumb. "Silly, aren't we?" She wiped a tear from her cheek, then blew her nose. "We ought to be going heavy on the protein, keeping up our strength. We're breaking our promise to him, fella, but it's sure hard trying to keep from fretting when we don't know what's happened."

She caught her breath as a persistent droning forced itself on her consciousness. Tumbleweed cocked his head, listening. Candles in glass holders had been placed on countertops and on the table to substitute for the light bulbs. By their flickering flames, she saw the dog bolt toward the back door, then jump against it in a frenzy.

Leigh snatched up one of the long flashlights she'd found in the supply cupboard.

In a flurry of motion she wrenched open the door and darted down the porch steps, the dog at her heels. The security system provided its own power, and Sentry had not been affected by the blackout. Now a warning light glowed on its control panel to indicate that a door had been left swinging wide. But Leigh, jubilant, didn't even notice. She was already dragging open the wrought-iron courtyard gate, straining her eyes for a better glimpse of the low-circling plane overhead.

"It's Carlos!" Her joyful cry merged with the steady drone of the engine. "Tumbleweed, he's back!"

Her short-sleeved blouse and linen slacks weren't nearly enough protection for the high desert climate once the sun went down, but Leigh paid no heed to the chilly night air. Without a plan in her head, she ran across the field, swinging the flashlight in wide circles to let Carlos know that he had found the right place.

Ten yards from the gate, her foot caught in a gopher hole, and she went sprawling across the hard-packed earth. She landed flat, the wind whooshing out of her on impact. Another inch to the side and she might have broken her ankle. She realized that such mindless behavior would hardly help to bring Carlos safely down.

The sun had sunk far past the western horizon; the feeble quarter moon had not yet risen. Carlos needed light, as much and as soon as possible. The power failure had rendered the double row of blue runway markers totally useless. It was going to be up to her, somehow, to round up enough illumination to help him land.

Scrambling to her feet, Leigh fumbled for the flashlight, which had rolled several feet away when she fell. Mercifully, it had escaped damage and glowed as brightly as ever.

It was so dark by now that all she could see of the plane was its single, bright round headlight and the winking red beacon on its wingtip. But Carlos had been circling and losing altitude with every turn.

She knew that with or without her help he meant to try a landing. An idea born of desperation occurred to Leigh. She swung the flashlight over her head in a dizzy bid for his attention. Then, switching it off and on in rapid clicks and wishing to heaven that she knew Morse code she directed its beam first toward the house, then back at the darkened runway. All she could do was hope he would realize she was trying to tell him something by this signal. If he would hold off, just for a minute, until she could bring help. . . .

It was now or never, Leigh realized. She had to make it fast. She had no idea what had delayed him en route or what his fuel situation was, but her instincts screamed at her that time was running out.

With the beam shining across the ground now to prevent another spill, she fled back through the gate and up the rear steps of the house. Placating Sentry took a few precious seconds. Then she was safely inside, tearing down the hall toward the guest quarters, shouting for the sisters to come and give her a hand.

"Quick! I need your help! Each of you grab a flashlight and run. Hurry!" she gasped as they dashed out of their rooms to meet her in the foyer. "Here — take this lantern while I grab my keys. Carlos is circling overhead. We've got to light up the runway so he can land."

After that, Leigh snatched the car keys out of her desk drawer, pushed the disengage button to shut off Sentry completely, and then sped out to the driveway where her Mustang was parked. Wrenching open the front door, she thrust the key into the ignition while the nuns piled in as fast as they could. Rubber burned in a black arcing circle as Leigh flipped the car into a wide U-turn, detoured around the courtyard wall, and plunged the front tires onto the open field.

Her headlights jiggled crazily, illuminating cactus, rocks, and sagebrush as she careened ahead. Keeping the accelerator floored, she steered around the largest of the obstacles in her path and mowed down the rest.

"There it is!" Sister Bernadette pointed to the long, slightly raised sweep of the runway. In a few words she outlined a simple plan to her companions. Leigh nodded agreement. She slowed the car to a crawl so that they could jump out.

Her worst worry now was getting mired in the desert's sandy loam. The rain that had passed over earlier had mostly run off, but an occasional slick puddle glinted as her headlights swept across it. As she pulled the wheel slightly to the right, she felt the tires bump and then catch on the first smooth surface since leaving the driveway.

Heading toward the end of the strip, she could see that one of the nuns had placed the lantern to mark the beginning of that dark sweep. Then, she and the others had spread out. Two women stood on each side of the long, straight stretch and held out their flashlights at arm's length, pointing the strong beams onto the tarmac to show Carlos where his plane could safely land.

Carlos had flown back and forth, his bright light winking in the sky, his turns assured as he dropped closer and closer to the ground. He saw the car reach the very end of the runway, then bump off the end and swing around. Its lights flooded back, reflecting on the farthest boundary of the airstrip. He knew that Leigh — all of them down there — were risking their own lives to bring him in.

It was dangerous. Foolhardy! But his gas tank was almost empty. If he tried to stretch it more than another mile or so, he was going to fall out of the sky.

Seat belt pinning him in place, he throttled down almost to stalling speed. One last time he checked that the flaps were down, that the gear was locked in place. Then he took careful aim at the lantern flickering at the head of the runway. Gently, carefully, he dipped the nose of the plane. He felt his wheels touch, bounce, touch again, and grip finally. The roar of the reverse thrust drowned even his thudding heartbeat as the plane hurtled past the courageously positioned nuns, their flashlights marking his limits left and right.

Brakes grabbed. Tires screeched across the wet, slick surface. Leigh waited dead ahead, counting on him to stop in time, her headlights flooding across the last few yards of the landing strip.

A wingtip swished through the yellow beam as Carlos swung the plane into a fast turn. The engine sputtered, consumed the last drop of fuel, and quit completely. The plane came to a vibrating halt in the middle of the runway.

The propeller gave one final rotation before fluttering to a standstill. There was a moment of absolute silence on the field while the scattered onlookers got their hearts out of their mouths and back down where they belonged. Then the cockpit door creaked open. As Carlos, looking exhausted, jumped to the ground, Leigh sprinted down the tarmac and hurled herself into his arms.

"Carlos! Oh, Carlos! I'm so happy to see you!"

Leigh hugged him to her chest, murmuring broken words of thanksgiving that he was back on the ground and safe. She could not hold back the tears of joy. They wet his cheek as well as her own.

Shuddering, Carlos folded her in a powerful embrace. He remembered her mad drive across the field. And her bravery at the end of the runway made him feel weak in the knees.

"I've never met anyone so brave," he said.

"Didn't it occur to you that I might run you down?"

She gave a small, nervous laugh. "You told me yourself that you were an awfully good pilot. And before you see the black tire tracks, I'd better confess that I burned rubber in reverse the entire length of the driveway. After this, I'll probably never be able to criticize you for being a speed demon again."

"Believe me, you won't have to. All reckless tendencies have been drained out of my system once and for all."

Carlos slackened his embrace as the four nuns scampered up to welcome him. He shook their hands and thanked them for their part in the rescue mission.

Moistness smarted at the corners of his eyes by the time he had finished. "I owe you all more than I can ever repay," he added with a backward glance at his immobile plane. "Do you know why that darned thing stopped where it did? It's out of gas. Without your help I would have been lost."

Sister Mary Jude beamed at him. "My dear young man, this night's adventure will turn out to be the highlight of our entire summer. You've given us a true dramatic experience that will keep our pupils enthralled for years to come!"

Each of the other nuns added a flurry of

congratulations for his superb handling of the plane under the most difficult of circumstances. Growing somewhat embarrassed by all the praise, Carlos was vastly relieved to hear an excited bark. He looked up to see Tumbleweed racing across the field toward him. Leaves clung to his pet's shaggy coat in several places, and the remains of an uprooted bush appeared to have fastened themselves to his tail. In his first enthusiastic dash toward the runway after Leigh had fallen and turned back to get her car, the dog had run afoul of the thorny desert shrubbery.

"Poor old guy! Looks like I'm not the only one to have survived a near-catastrophe tonight!" Carlos wrapped his faithful friend in a glad hug. While someone retrieved the lantern, he rid Tumbleweed's coat of the worst burrs and clumps of foliage. Then the whole group made their way back to Leigh's car.

The return trip to the house seemed slow and bumpy compared to their furious cross-country trek before. This time the tires, springs, and shock absorbers advised the Mustang's passengers of every pothole, molehill, rock, or spiny cactus they jounced across. By the time they reached the pavement, Leigh's hands were trembling from the effort of holding the wheel on course.

"My adrenaline probably won't stop bubbling for hours," she declared, pulling into the driveway and setting the hand brake. "I think we could all use something to eat."

Still excited, the nuns crowded into the kitchen with her. A big pot of coffee was set on the gas stove to perk. By candlelight, plates of ham and cheese sandwiches were prepared and a carton of deli potato salad was unearthed from the depths of the refrigerator.

While all this was going on, Carlos dropped wearily into his desk chair. Lantern flickering nearby, he reached for the telephone. He called Serita first, assuring her that he was safely home at last and asking her to have the search called off. Having promised to fill her in on all the details tomorrow, he hung up and notified the air-traffic controllers at the local field that he had made a safe emergency landing.

By the time he got back to the kitchen, the makeshift dinner was ready. In between bites, Carlos described the final tense stage of his flight.

"I made an approach from the southeast. When I didn't see any lights where I knew darned well Santa Fe ought to be, I radioed the control tower. They gave me the word about the blackout, and suggested I head for Albuquerque, a very short distance. But I was so low on fuel that I doubted I could make it. I figured I'd better take my chances with my own private strip, lights or no lights."

Leigh carried over the coffeepot for refills. Carlos gave her a squeeze and reached for another sandwich.

"I saw your signals with the flashlight, Leigh — pointing to the house, then over to the runway. I figured you had something up your sleeve, though I never dreamed of it being the dramatic act you pulled. So I decided to circle as long as possible to give you a chance to do your best."

And to use up the rest of his fuel, Carlos added to himself. He had wanted there to be a minimum of high octane gasoline left in his tank to go up in flame should the crash landing go wrong. No point mentioning anything about that worry now, though. It was all behind them.

When they were alone at last, he held Leigh in his arms, cradling his tired head on her shoulder. "What a heroine you are, *querida*," he said. "Please don't ever lay your life on the line for anyone again, not even for me."

She would of course, Leigh knew. The same as he would for her. That was what love was all about. She caressed his cheek with her hand. "I'd be lying if I tried to deceive you and say I wasn't worried."

"You're forgiven this time. I was scared to death up there," Carlos admitted. "Maybe I was wrong, making you promise not to stew over me. Sometimes there's just no help for it."

"Yes, but on the other hand we've proved that by working together we can overcome a great obstacle."

It wasn't until later that Leigh heard the full story of what had caused the long delay in her Carlos's return flight.

After leaving Dallas, the trip had been strictly routine for the first two-thirds of the way. Then, without warning, the oil pressure gauge had started doing crazy things again. Its readout was so erratic that he realized he would never make the last two hundred miles home unless he could regulate the faulty mechanism.

"Naturally, that happened while I was flying over an area of deep gorges and heavily timbered hills," he recollected. "Then all of a sudden I caught sight of this marvelous mesa dead ahead — flat as a pancake and not a twig in sight. I wasn't about to argue with luck like that. I called off a Mayday — a distress call and started down. If anyone picked it up, I didn't hear them respond.

Things were happening pretty quickly. I couldn't wait around for an acknowledgment."

He'd made the unscheduled landing at about midday. Once down, it seemed to take forever for his engine to cool enough so that he could work on it. Afterward he got busy, using the tools he always carried along. He ripped one of his spare shirts into cleaning rags and tackled the repair job.

"I might have been imagining things, but the howling coyotes seemed to get closer and closer as the day went on. The idea of spending the night on the mesa, surrounded by a pack of hungry animals, was hardly to my liking. It would have been safe enough inside the plane, I suppose. Still, I knew you'd be worried if I didn't show up. And Serita too. She's a good kid in spite of the problems we've been having lately. I got the idea she might have been getting fed up with Cahill. He kept trying to back the two of us into a corner and she didn't go for that any more than I did. The weather forecast advised that the storm would have been long gone from Santa Fe by noon. It must have been close to six-thirty when I got back into the air. Of course, I didn't know about the blackout until I was practically on top of the town."

The sight of the darkened city had nearly

thrown him for a loop, Carlos admitted. The commercial field was closed; his fuel was insufficient to reach Albuquerque.

Carlos grinned. "So here I am, thanks to you and our four good friends." He realized now that landing on the mesa and then taking off from there must have used up more of his reserve gasoline than he had suspected at the time. Nevertheless, he intended to have the fuel tank checked for leaks as soon as possible.

During the night the power was restored. Carlos rang up the local airfield before breakfast. By nine, a crew of mechanics had arrived to give the plane a thorough servicing.

The team worked painstakingly for several hours. The gasoline tank was checked and double-checked. Any gauges or engine parts showing the slightest amount of wear were replaced. The rest of the machinery was cleaned and retested while the body of the aircraft itself was gone over from nose to tail.

Grease gun in hand, a mechanic crawled underneath the plane for a routine inspection of the landing gear. Suddenly, his muffled voice drifted back to the others: "What in tarnation is this thing?"

Carlos, who had been working with the crew, wiggled under the plane to see what the mechanic was talking about. The mechanic pointed to a small, square box mounted inconspicuously just behind the wheel wells. "I hate to admit my ignorance," he said, "but I'm not sure what the function of this gadget is."

"Don't feel bad," Carlos said grimly. "I don't know either, and I've been flying around with the darned thing for quite some time now, apparently."

He wiped his gritty fingers on a rag and traced the outline of the box. Someone had gone to a lot of trouble to keep it from being noticed, because the metal casing had been painted the same color as the belly of the airplane, and it was recessed behind the undercarriage where it was least likely to be spotted. Only during a complete overhaul would anyone have seen it and begun to wonder.

Leigh, accompanying Tumbleweed on his noontime romp, walked up to find all the mechanics scowling at the sophisticated piece of gadgetry. She eyed it with suspicion, and suggested that they ask Kit to check it out.

"Airplanes aren't his specialty, but I can't think of anyone with more expertise in microcircuitry," she went on. "Sentry and his other inventions run on electronic chips and tiny computer modules. If Kit can't identify that thing, he could probably make an educated guess as to what it's used for."

"Let's call him right now," Carlos said.

The crew knocked off for lunch while Leigh phoned Kit. Fortunately, he was able to come right away. "What a beauty," he said reverently, with the appreciation of an expert technician for a piece of intricate workmanship.

"I'm glad you think so," Carlos grumbled. "But what is it for? I'll be interested to learn what it's doing on my plane."

After detaching the device, Kit transferred it onto a piece of clean toweling. He removed the top plate, then proceeded to prod at the interior with a miniature screwdriver. Peering over his shoulder, Carlos and Leigh eyed the swirling bundles of multicolored wires and the tiny lines with which the instrument was calibrated. Though they were obviously anxious to have the answer, Kit took his time, subjecting the box to a careful series of tests before setting aside his tools and looking up at them.

"To put it in layman's terms, what you have here, my friend, is a bug," he announced. "Someone has been tracking you around the sky!"

Chapter Nine

The three of them stared down at the mysterious box that had been attached to the underside of Carlos's plane.

"It's an electronic homing device," Kit explained. "Somewhere there has to be a compatible receptor on which the aircraft's movements are monitored and charted."

Carlos looked thunderstruck. "Do you mean to say that someone has been having me followed?"

"That's about the size of it," Kit said somberly. He tapped the tough outer casing of the mechanism. "This is an expensive piece of space-age hardware. I wouldn't be surprised if it has a range of five hundred miles or more. Anyone interested in keeping tabs on you can just flip a switch and watch your plane blip across a screen."

He said that the trackers wouldn't need to be airborne, though that was a possibility. The scanner could be mounted in a truck as easily as in a helicopter.

"The beauty of it, from their point of view, is that they'd never have to give the show away by coming anywhere near you. The readout from the instrumentation would tell them everything they needed to know. You would never realize you were being spied upon."

"That must be the explanation!" Leigh cried.

Carlos looked ready to spit nails. "You bet it is! This is exactly how my discoveries were snatched away from me. For months I've been going out of my head trying to figure out how anyone could possibly know where I've been and what I've found, let alone how they managed to sneak in and register the claim ahead of me. But now there isn't any doubt about how they worked it."

Carlos shoved back a lock of hair that had dropped across his forehead. A streak of grease marked his temple. There was a smudge on his jaw, and his hands and clothing showed the effects of the morning's work. Gazing at his slim, straight form, Leigh thought she had never seen a more appealing man. The fiery temper of his Spanish ancestors had put a flinty spark in his dark eyes, and his lean jaw bulged with righteous indignation. It was a good thing his adversary wasn't anywhere near by just then. He would have been stretched out on the ground in nothing flat!

Kit knew nothing of the professional woes that had been plaguing the petro-geologist. Quickly, they filled him in on the maddening situation.

"Most of my oil exploring is done by plane," Carlos finished. "Since last May I've made two or three very promising discoveries. Each time, the find was pirated right out from under my nose. It didn't seem possible that such a thing could keep happening. But it did."

Kit pointed to a miniature wireless transmitter. "See that? It would give them a constant feedback of hard information. Latitude, longitude, altitude — anything they wanted to know about your position. It would also clock the time you spent on the ground. Then, once you had taken off and left the area, it would pinpoint your exact landing point. From what you've said, I suspect they'd have moved in fast, scooped up soil samples, snapped a few photos, and mapped out the boundaries. Then off they'd zoom to register the area's mineral rights. They would be filing the claim almost before you made it home and got your wheels chocked."

A suspicion had been growing in Leigh's mind while she listened to the men's discussion. She said, "Kit, would you have any way of telling how long that thing has been on the plane?"

He used a magnifying glass to examine the exterior casing. "Judging from the shape it's in, six months at the most. If it had been there during the winter, rust or corrosion would have set in."

When they both eyed Leigh with curiosity, she explained the theory that had occurred to her: "Carlos, you flew down to Dallas last Easter to visit Serita. She introduced you to her new boyfriend. At the time, you said, Denny Cahill seemed very enthusiastic about your plane. He crawled all over it, and even mentioned taking flying lessons himself."

"That's it!" Carlos crashed a fist into the palm of his other hand. "I should have guessed he was up to something, especially after a friend of his drew me aside in the hangar and asked a lot of long-winded questions. There would have been plenty of time for Cahill to slip underneath my plane right then and mount that equipment."

"You told me that some low-profile corporation had filed the claims on your discoveries," Leigh said. "Would there be any way to find out if Denny Cahill is connected with that company?"

"It's sure worth a try." Carlos glared at the device Kit was holding. "Maybe I'll never be able to prove who bugged my plane, but now that I know how the claims were jumped, I may be able to persuade a judge to issue an injunction and at least force that outfit to reveal the names of its officers." He looked up in grim satisfaction. "If we can link Cahill to the company, it will show Serita what sort of *bandito* she's been engaged to! That would be a victory in itself."

The more he thought it over, the more convinced Carlos became that Denny Cahill had gotten wind of his prospecting expeditions in advance.

"I usually kept Serita posted on where I was going and how long I'd be away, so that she could contact me in case of emergency," he explained. "That swindler could have gotten the information without my sister's having any idea she was spilling a secret."

There was no longer any doubt as to how the thefts had been accomplished. And though no legal proof against Denny Cahill had yet been found, at least Carlos's future discoveries would be safe — from that sort of piracy. Leigh smiled as an amusing thought occurred to her.

"Too bad that crook didn't flip on his homing device during your return trip to Santa Fe," she said. "When you came down on that mesa, he might have figured you had landed on purpose to check out some exciting discovery."

Carlos smiled too. "You know, it's not impossible that that *might* have happened. I didn't want to make it look as if my only motive for flying down to Dallas was to play the part of the tightfisted older brother. It seems to me I said something about deciding to mix business with pleasure."

"You mentioned that your sister and her fiancé had been bickering," Leigh said. "When Serita drove you to the airport yesterday morning, she knew you intended to come straight home. But chances are, she wouldn't have said anything about your plans to him. All he would know was your approximate departure time. If he activated the homing gadget and followed your. . . ."

Carlos was laughing now. "Wouldn't it be a kick if he pinpointed that bare mesa as my latest discovery? Tinkering with that blasted gauge took me most of the afternoon. But someone who had me on radar, and who couldn't see that I was up to my elbows in grease, might have figured that I spent those six hours probing the soil for signs of a petroleum deposit."

"Wouldn't that just serve him right!" Kit cried. "I've seen some of those bare, windswept mesas. They're good for absolutely nothing except great background scenery for Western movies." A crafty look crept over his face. "Anyone who staked a claim to that kind of landscape would be the joke of the oil industry. Could you find out if a claim has been registered?"

"Sure thing." Carlos hurried into the house to place a long-distance call. A few minutes later he emerged wearing a wide, triumphant grin.

"I wouldn't have believed anyone could be that gullible! At nine o'clock this morning, a claim for the mineral rights on that mesa was registered by the same wily corporation that's been plaguing me all along!"

"We may be able to turn the tables on this weasel without applying for an injunction," Kit said. "Embarrassment and humiliation are mighty potent weapons. It just so happens that my brother Jack is a reporter for one of the big dailies down in Fort Worth. If word of this incident should happen to trickle into the newspaper sort of by accident. . . .

"The entire corporation would have egg on its face," Leigh predicted.

"And I'll bet their stockholders would be none too pleased to learn that their capital is being used to drill as deep as China before any oil showed up from that big find." Carlos chimed in. "Denny Cahill would have to move quickly to avoid being fired and sued."

Leigh agreed that feelings had been known to run high among oil speculators. "You couldn't have arranged a better sting if you'd spent a month plotting it out with a team of con men," she said, giggling. "Let's make sure Jack gets every single detail. If he doesn't win the Pulitzer Prize for his story, he ought to at least come up with a raise for his clever investigative reporting!"

Within a week Leigh's prediction had come true. Jack Martindale's article hit the front page of the Fort Worth *Times*. National newspapers soon picked up the story and a major magazine exposé followed. Jack earned a promotion. Denny Cahill was laughed out of town and out of the oil industry.

At that, he proved to have made a lucky getaway, because soon afterward, a committee of engineers from Texas A and M took a close look at the new oil pump Cahill had been trying to get Serita to finance and termed it a totally worthless contrivance. "Fraud" was one of the milder terms used to describe his activities.

In Leigh's opinion, this comeuppance was exactly what Denny Cahill deserved. There was no telling how many other people he had cheated and deceived. Though she felt sorry for Serita, she believed that her future sister-in-law had had a narrow escape.

Serita was holding her chin high when she came back to Santa Fe at the end of August. She admitted that her heart was bruised, but far from broken. "Just think!" she exclaimed. "I might have married that crook and let him swindle me out of my inheritance. It cost Jimmi Haviland a pretty penny to be rid of him."

Carlos turned aside to conceal a smile. That was exactly what he had tried to tell Serita, but for months she had refused to listen. Experience had certainly proved to be a good teacher!

Leigh kept a straight face with no difficulty. She knew what an effort it must have been for Serita to come right out and admit that she had misjudged the man. After hearing that Denny Cahill had shown up in Rio de Janeiro, Leigh observed, "I understand that in South America, fathers and brothers are very quick to avenge any slurs on their family honor. Denny is going to find it difficult to sweet-talk any more young heiresses to see things his way — not without living to regret it."

"Yes, he may actually have to get an honest job," Serita sniped. "Speaking of jobs, I've applied for a position with the United Nations in New York. I've had lots of experience translating from English to Spanish and back again. Portuguese too. I know several delegations that would be glad to have me."

"It will be a wonderful new experience, seeing the East and working with people from all over the world," Leigh said enthusiastically. "But I hope you aren't planning to go until after October tenth!"

Serita gave her a hug. "Don't worry. I wouldn't miss your wedding for anything. I'm so glad you're going to marry my brother!"

Leigh had moved back to her own apartment in town soon after the discovery of the homing device on the plane. By the time Serita arrived for an extended visit, the nuns had left, going their separate ways in preparation for the coming school year. Carlos and Serita should spend a little time getting reacquainted, Leigh thought. Besides, this way Serita would be on hand to welcome their parents when they flew in from Australia. Then, as soon as Ines and her family arrived from Alaska, the family would be temporarily complete once again.

But that wouldn't be happening for more than a month yet. Meanwhile, they all had their hands full. Between business and preparations for the wedding, there didn't seem to be a spare minute.

Though Sitting Tight had a satisfactory number of bookings for the autumn months, summer had been the little company's peak season. Even so, Leigh was already penciling in reservations for the holiday weeks. Her house-sitters were in great demand between Thanksgiving and New Year's.

"I'm really glad things slack off a bit this time of year," she told Roger, who was assisting her part-time in the office these days. In addition to being an excellent researcher, the historian had also turned out to be a competent accountant. Leigh had gratefully turned all her bookkeeping chores over to him. Little by little, the debt for the towing charges and the repairs to his van were being worked off. She considered the trade more than a fair exchange.

He looked up from the calculator. "I can see your point. If we were *really* busy, when would you have time to try on the contents of all those fancy boxes you keep dragging in here every noontime?"

"I've done a little trousseau shopping." Leigh shrugged airily. "So what?"

"Just don't expect me to help you get all those invitations out at the last minute."

"They're already finished," she said, and heaved a grateful sigh that this chore, at least, was finally complete. "Gail and Serita and I spent every evening last week addressing and stamping them. They went out in yesterday's mail." She looped her leather shoulder bag over her arm. "I may be a little late getting back from lunch today. I want to spend a little time with Gail. She's close to her delivery date now, and Kit can't be there with her every minute."

As it turned out, Kit was the very first person she set eyes on when she pulled up to the curb in front of their apartment house. He was loping down the front walk looking more than a little frantic.

"Leigh! Am I glad to see you!" He pulled open her car door and helped her out. She noted with wonder that his fingers were trembling. "Gail is sitting inside clutching her middle, and that dimwitted kid I hired to help me with deliveries is still off somewhere with the van. I was just about to hail a taxi."

"No need for that. I'll be happy to drive," she volunteered promptly. "You run back and help Gail, and let me handle her suitcase."

She found her friend all set to go. "I'll be fine, you guys," Gail said. "Quit fussing."

The mother-to-be was far calmer than her husband. Nevertheless, it was a relief to Leigh to pull in to the hospital's emergency entrance and find efficient people waiting with a wheelchair to escort Gail up to the maternity floor.

The insurance papers had been prepared in advance, but there were still admittance forms to be filled out and various other bits of red tape to be unsnarled. To Kit's everlasting gratitude, Leigh stayed to help him. What with all the confusion, it was well past three o'clock before she remembered to call Roger and let him know where she was.

"Is your friend okay?" He knew how anxious she had been lately.

"Yes. At least, I think so." Leigh found herself crossing her fingers. Gail had an excellent doctor, but even so. . . . "Unless you really need me there, I think I'll just stay here the rest of the day."

"Good idea," Roger agreed. "This office is too darned small for two people, anyhow. I'll lock up at five and see you tomorrow."

Leigh wound up staying at the hospital through the dinner hour. For friendship's sake, Kit agreed to leave the waiting room long enough to accompany her down to the cafeteria. There, she managed to coax him into swallowing a few bites of supper. Then he insisted on sending her home.

The next morning, while she was getting dressed for work, her phone rang. She answered it, and found herself talking to a proud new father.

"Congratulations, Auntie!" Kit exulted. "You have two beautiful nieces. Our twin daughters arrived about half an hour ago."

Leigh was so excited that for a moment she couldn't manage to form coherent words. "How wonderful! Fan-fantastic! Are they both okay? And Gail? Is she all right?"

"Everyone's perfect!"

"I can't wait to see the babies," Leigh bubbled. "What are their names?"

"I'll introduce you officially in person. Visiting hours this afternoon are between two and four. Can you come for a quick peek then?"

"Just try to keep me away!"

That afternoon, Leigh learned why the new parents had conspired to keep the babies' names a secret. Taking her hand when she got off the elevator at the third floor, Kit led her down the hall to a glass-enclosed nursery. From the corridor viewing window, they were granted a quick glimpse of a tiny new human being.

"Leigh, meet Leigh Anne," Kit said proudly. "That's her baby sister in the next bassinet. Christina Gail arrived ten minutes later."

"Oh, Kit!" Leigh was so touched that she could hardly speak. She had never felt so honored in her entire life. "You named the baby after *me?*"

"Yes, because you're so totally special to both of us." He gave her a hug. "Gail and I are so glad you've found Carlos, sweetheart. Love's wonderful, isn't it? From now on, the future's coming up roses for all of us."

While washing the tearstains from her face in the ladies' room a few minutes later, Leigh crossed her fingers that Kit's prediction would come true. Carlos was a wonderful, dependable person. He loved her as much as she loved him. But she was never quite able to forget that she'd once had a father who had seemed to love her too. Yet he had walked away and never returned.

Annoyed at herself for thinking of anything so demoralizing on such a happy day, she summoned her best smile, then rejoined Kit in the corridor. A moment later he was ushering her into Gail's room.

She took her friend's hand in both of hers. "Congratulations on a fantastic job," she murmured, thinking how tired yet proud Gail looked. "You really outdid yourself. They're adorable."

"Of course. Did you expect anything less? They're going to be carrot-tops like their Dad." A smile flickered across Gail's face. "What did you think of our surprise?"

Leigh grew misty-eyed. "Having a baby named after me was the biggest compliment I've ever received."

"We've all been so close, dearer to one another than the most devoted brother and sisters. Like the Three Musketeers. It seemed only right that the babies should be named for the three of us."

" 'All for one and one for all.' " Bending over the bed, Leigh gave her friend a loving hug. "You've made me very happy and proud. Now I want you to rest while I call Carlos and tell him the wonderful news. We'll both see you later."

That evening, Carlos arrived at the hospital with two spectacular bouquets. Gail had slept for most of the day. Now she was sitting up in bed wearing a pretty quilted bed jacket. Her long hair had been brushed until it gleamed, and there was a very contented smile on her face.

"You're looking positively radiant," Carlos said after he had pumped Kit's hand and kissed Gail on the cheek. "If your two daughters grow up looking half as pretty as their mother, Sentry will have a full-time job shooing away their admirers."

After leaving the hospital, he steered Leigh into the first decent restaurant he spotted. "I suspect that what with all the excitement of the past couple of days, you've been skipping meals." His arm slid around her waist. Always slender, it was even more so now. "If this keeps up, we'll have to tie weights to the hem of your wedding dress. Floating down the aisle is one thing, and I know I'm marrying an angel, but even so. . . ."

Leigh laughed at his foolishness, but humored him by tucking into her steak with gusto. She and Gail were the luckiest girls in Santa Fe, she thought. Thin or plump, it made no difference. They were loved.

Later that week Carlos left town for several days of desert exploring. It was a routine part of his profession, but Leigh had expected to feel a brooding anxiety every minute he was gone. However, she was able to wave him off with equanimity. It was a relief to find that she could go calmly ahead with her business while he was tending to his.

Carlos found it very reassuring to realize that his fiancée had the utmost confidence in his ability as a pilot. All too vividly he remembered the trauma of landing in a blackout with her courageous help. He decided that having come through that crisis, she had realized there was nothing to worry about in the future. They would enjoy their time together, cope during separations, and celebrate every reunion like no other two people had ever done before.

Though the unexplored geological formations he'd had his eye on for some months proved interesting, he found no signs of a potential oil field beneath the strata. Having looked forward to an exciting find, he was a little disappointed. He might just as well have checked it out earlier, when Denny Cahill's tracking device was snatching away his discoveries before they could be recorded.

Turning back for another careful examination, he confirmed his original decision. There was no oil here. On the other hand. . . . Scowling thoughtfully at the formations, he logged the coordinates in his pocket notebook with the utmost care. He wanted to be able to find this place again. On his next expedition, he'd bring along a Geiger counter.

His suspicion that uranium lay beneath the earth he had just been examining reminded Carlos of something that had been troubling him for months now. He had made one attempt to look into it, but so far nothing had come of his idea. He decided that the time

182

had come for another try at learning the truth.

As soon as he returned to Santa Fe, he called up and made an appointment. That same afternoon he dropped by the local convent for a visit with the Mother Superior.

"It's possible your guess was right," his aunt told him. "There have been rumors trickling down from the north. But as yet I can't tell you anything for sure." When a bell rang, she stood up briskly and ushered him out of her office. "The invitation to your wedding arrived last week," she said with a smile. "Leigh sounds like a lovely girl."

"She is," Carlos said. "I'm looking forward to being her husband. But I'd like to get this matter settled before we exchange rings. It could mean a lot to her. To both of us."

"Yes, I can see why it would," his aunt agreed. "Let me write another letter. I'll get in touch with you as soon as I receive a reply."

Chapter Ten

September passed in a blur of activity. Leigh had never been so busy. Or so happy. Every time she saw Carlos she fell more deeply in love with him. They went out frequently in the evenings. On Sundays, she usually spent the day at his house, where she had a chance to romp with Tumbleweed and become better acquainted with Serita.

Several times a week she also managed a visit to the Martindale home. In spite of the addition of infant twins to the household, things were running very smoothly there. Leigh marveled at the way a good marriage such as Kit and Gail's could continue to grow even better day by day. She hoped to have the same thing happen with Carlos and herself.

The babies seemed to have grown in just the three weeks since their birth. Playing no favorites, Leigh enjoyed cuddling them both, and discovering new ways to tell them apart. She didn't mind pitching in to change diapers or hold a fretful child. She became quite expert at patting a tiny back until a giant moist burp split the air.

"Practicing for when you have your own?" Gail laughed at the outrageous noise issuing from her dainty daughter.

"You bet," Leigh said. "Carlos and I hope to have a houseful of burpy babies ourselves someday. Just one at a time, though. I don't see how you have hands enough to take care of twins."

"I must confess I'm relieved not to have produced triplets. But we would have managed." Beginning to puff a bit, Gail bent forward and touched her toes with outstretched fingers. "But I'd probably be working off six additional inches if I'd been eating for four instead of only for three."

She continued with the sit-ups she did faithfully twice a day. The dress they had chosen for her matron-of-honor role was a beautiful, frothy creation of yellow chiffon. She was hoping to fit into the same size she had worn before her pregnancy, but tightening her tummy muscles was proving to be uphill work.

Regarding the wedding, the exact size of Gail's dress was one of the very few arrangements still in doubt. Serita had proved to be a tireless organizer. Leigh, suspecting that her future sister-in-law needed an occupation to take her mind off her own broken engagement, had gladly turned over to her a great many of the most time-consuming details. Thanks to efficient planning, the church and reception hall were reserved, an organist had been hired, and the caterer, florist, and photographer were poised to do their parts come October tenth.

Reservations for a romantic, two-week honeymoon on a Caribbean island were already confirmed too. The only cloud in this silver lining was Sitting Tight. Leigh mentally crossed her fingers whenever she thought about leaving Roger and Angelina jointly in charge of her business.

"They'll do fine while we're away," Carlos predicted. "However, I do think a weekend trial run to get the bugs out of their teamwork would be a wise idea. Roger can practice rounding up replacement house-sitters so he can go out and chase down a legend, and Angelina can tongue-lash him into staying put."

"You've summed up their major character traits in a nutshell."

Leigh laughed, though just the thought of the lackadaisical historian and the querulous science major sharing that cramped office of hers conjured up nightmares. But a glance at her fiancé told her that his suggestion had not been made in jest.

"You were serious, weren't you?"

He nodded. "Absolutely. Running your own business is fine, but you have to learn to let go once in a while. Here's your chance. Turn the key over to Roger and Angelina and walk away. Don't give them another thought until Monday. I have an outing all planned for Saturday, and have even rented a Jeep."

There was an oddly anxious look in his eyes, and Leigh suspected that his tension was in some way related to this mysterious weekend he was urging her to share.

"Will you come, Leigh?" he prodded. "String along with me and not ask too many questions?"

Only once before had Carlos asked for blind trust from her. That was when he insisted that she must not worry about him while he was in the air. She had agreed then, and even though that one emergency landing had strained her faith, it had turned out all right. This outing, whatever it involved, must be very important to him.

That was good enough for her. They were going to be a team, for better or for worse. There was no time like the present to start practicing that philosophy.

"Sure, I'll come." She mustered a confident smile for him. "Just tell me when to be ready and what to wear. From that reference to a Jeep, I gather we aren't just going to run up to Taos to browse through the art galleries, are we?"

"Not this time," Carlos said, relaxing somewhat. "Let's plan on getting started at about six in the morning. Wear jeans and a light shirt, but bring a warm jacket too. And, uh, snakeproof boots might not be a bad idea, either."

Leigh swallowed a groan. She liked snakes even less than she did bookkeeping, and avoided their haunts whenever possible. Somehow, it didn't sound like Carlos had planned a terribly entertaining field trip.

Why in the world was he so set on going *now*, less than two weeks before their wedding? Lucky for him, she'd given her word not to ask any more questions than were absolutely necessary.

For the first two hours of the journey, Leigh huddled inside her jacket. She was thankful for the warm protection of the tough outer denim and its cozy sheepskin lining. At around eight o'clock she peeled off her mittens and poured cups of coffee from a steaming thermos. They took the opportunity to stretch their legs while gulping down the reviving brew. But Carlos seemed anxious to get going again. Five minutes later they were back in the Jeep, traveling northeast at a moderate but steady pace.

Business, squabbling employees, even her anxiety over meeting the rest of his family slipped from Leigh's mind as she relaxed beside him on the jouncing seat. Now that they were underway she was content to simply sit back and enjoy the scenery and the company of the man she loved. She had to admit, though, that the question of where they were headed — and why — had given her more than one puzzling moment over the past forty-eight hours.

An hour or so out of Santa Fe they had veered off the main highway. In Leigh's opinion, the bumpy mountain road they were following now would have rated no more than a thin gray line on a map. The route had its hazards. Detours around piles of fallen rock were common. So were terrifying hairpin curves. But she found the glimpses of the fertile valleys of the Rio Grande far below to be breathtakingly beautiful.

Carlos really was an excellent driver, she thought, noticing the sure and steady grip his strong hands maintained on the wheel.

The increasing altitude gave her a lightheaded feeling. She welcomed his suggestion that they pause for food at a roadside picnic area beyond Ojo Sarco. While she spread a cloth over the rough table, he hauled out a cooler that Serita had packed with goodies for them. Together they set out biscuits, a jar of honey, and thick slices of ham. Rummaging further, Leigh found a bottle of green olives and six hard-boiled eggs. She placed them beside the six-pack of soda that Carlos had unearthed from beneath a blanket of ice cubes.

She removed her jacket, rolled up the sleeves of her plaid shirt, and prepared to dig in. "Wow!" she exclaimed. "When the Wainwright family provides food, they don't do things by halves!"

"We don't do anything by halves." Carlos wrapped his arms around her, drawing her close for a kiss that demonstrated exactly what he meant.

He soon released her, though, and turned aside to fill a paper plate with food. Leigh noticed that he wasn't eating with his usual enthusiasm, though. Apprehension shivered across the back of her neck. If Carlos had lost his appetite, something must be terribly wrong.

She longed to put her foot down and demand a few straight answers. But a promise was a promise. Edgily, Leigh policed the area for litter while Carlos hoisted the heavy ice chest back into the Jeep. She was growing more and more anxious to reach their destination, so that she could find out what in the world was going on.

For two hours longer they rumbled up one hill and down the next, climbing steadily. Leigh was thoroughly sick of this rugged landscape by now. But when Carlos pulled over to the side of the road without warning and cut the engine, she was more surprised than pleased.

"What's the matter? We aren't out of gas, are we?"

"Don't you trust me?" He sounded cross and nervous. "Nothing's the matter at all. We're almost there. I wanted to talk with you for a minute before we went any farther, that's all. Hop out."

Leigh did as he asked. A deep, open valley glided off below. Ahead were peaks of the Sangre de Cristo Mountains, snowcapped the year round. As far as she could tell, they were smack in the middle of nowhere.

Before she could think of a tactful way to bring this to his attention, Carlos pointed to something a mile or two off. "Look down there."

Totally bewildered, Leigh followed the direction of his pointing finger. Then her eyes widened. She had almost missed it!

So neutrally clay-colored that in fading light it would have merged entirely with the dun tones of the background cliffs, an unusual settlement sprawled below. In the noontime glare Leigh saw a large cluster of attached houses, most of which rose four or five stories high. The square adobe structures, with their narrow windows and skylight entrances, had been intricately terraced. The roofs of the lower group of rooms served as porches for the story above.

"A pueblo!" Leigh had no trouble recognizing the apartment-type housing that cliff-dwelling Native Americans had been occupying since long before the Spaniards' arrival in the New World. "I've never been so close to one before."

"Here's your chance for a visit."

She stared at him in astonishment. "Oh, but they wouldn't allow it."

"Yes, they would. As a matter of fact, we're expected."

He sounded calm, she thought, but he looked positively stiff with tension. "Carlos, I don't understand any of this," she said. "Have you been here before?"

"Last Monday. I didn't want to tell you anything about it in advance because it was meant to be a surprise. Honest, Leigh, there's nothing to worry about. It all came about because of an idea I've been mulling over for several months. Not too long ago, I enlisted some help, and asked a certain group of people to keep their eyes and ears open."

"And they did? They found an answer you had been looking for?"

He nodded. "That's it. Someone got in touch with me, and I drove out here to check it out. There was a certain amount of protocol involved. My informant acted as go-between. She introduced me to Niza. He's sort of the chief of this village. Here the people use the Keresan dialect, and he let me know that we were on his home ground by using only that language. Our conversation had to be translated back and forth from Keresan into English. But today we won't need an interpreter. Niza has agreed to speak with us directly in Spanish."

Because of the centuries of Spanish influence in the Southwest, many of the more remote tribes were more familiar with that language than English. Though aware of this, Leigh still found the situation baffling. She knew that Carlos was able to speak several Indian dialects, and that this fact had been a help in his work. But today's trip wasn't anything professional. And she felt certain that she herself was somehow involved.

She didn't know which seemed odder to her, the fact that Carlos's go-between was a woman or that this important man called Niza had condescended to speak with *her* at all, let alone in Spanish.

What in the world was going on?

Taking her hand, Carlos led the way back to the Jeep. "I saw a couple of kids down there playing lookout. People will know that we're on the way. Let's not keep them waiting."

Leigh had the strangest impression that she was keeping a date with destiny. Carlos seemed very grave. He, too, seemed to feel that something vitally important was taking place. Though she trusted him, Leigh didn't feel the least bit comfortable. She thought of Roger and his fascination with ancient legends, then pushed the notion firmly out of her mind. Whatever this concerned was real, not myth.

Before reaching the outskirts of the pueblo, Carlos slowed the Jeep almost to a crawl. Even so, plumes of dust whirled from beneath the tires. Leigh was too engrossed by their strange surroundings to notice.

Defense, she remembered, had been the first priority of a pueblo. The cliff dwellers were peaceful people who had banded together for safety's sake. Many hundreds of years ago, when this desert skyscraper was originally constructed, no doors or windows would have been cut in the thick adobe ground-level walls. People living there would have used ladders to climb to the lowest rooftop, then have entered their homes through openings in the ceiling. How dark and gloomy it must have been inside, she thought.

If an enemy attacked, the ladders could be hoisted and the pueblo turned into an impregnable fortress. That's why the place had survived for so long. Leigh saw that the ladders still served a useful function. They were propped up in various spots alongside the walls for the convenience of those living on the higher levels of the structure. But the ground-floor rooms were no longer closed boxes. Modern-day residents had added blue-trimmed doors and windows to their homes.

As they parked the Jeep and climbed slowly out, Leigh noticed several beehive-shaped ovens taller than her head. These were separated from the main buildings. A plump woman was pushing loaves of bread into one of the huge ovens with a long-handled shovel. Nearby, a slim, pretty teenager wielded a broom vigorously.

Playing tag, happy children ran barefoot

through the street. Most of the men and youths of the pueblo appeared to be busy in the fields. Across the road an expanse of dried cornstalks rattled in the breeze. That crop had been harvested for the year, but immense pumpkins, squash, and other fall vegetables were still ripening in the blazing sun.

Carlos ushered her past the living quarters and a rectangular one-story building called a *kiva*. This, he said, was a ceremonial chamber used only by the men of the tribe. A second such room was open to all the local people. As they stepped inside, a middle-aged man came forward. He was dressed in denims and a plaid shirt, with a colorful band twisted around his forehead. His black eyes flickered curiously across Leigh's face, but he addressed himself to Carlos.

"Wait here," he said in Spanish. "I will bring Niza."

It was refreshingly cool inside due to the thick insulation of the adobe walls. Leigh guessed that this communal room was probably used for meetings as well as a workshop for the traditional crafts. Basketry took up one corner, and a few exquisite examples of the cane worker's art were stacked on a shelf. A table held others that were scarcely begun.

She was even more interested in the pottery she spotted on the opposite side of the room. To quell her growing nervousness, she studied the pottery closely. The pieces were of various sizes and shapes, painted in several precise designs. White, black, and the same pale blue used to outline the pueblo's doors and windows were enlivened by an occasional splash of red. She wondered whether one of the big baking ovens outside also served as a kiln to fire the clay.

By the time the tribesman reappeared, she was ready to bite her fingernails. Leigh saw him approach the door, then stand deferentially aside to allow a much older man to enter first.

This was a person of authority, she knew. His bearing and dignity testified to his rank. Though his brown skin had crumpled into an intricate network of wrinkles, his shoulders were still straight. Not a single strand of silver was visible in his long black braids.

Carlos stepped forward, and, extending his hand, he greeted Niza in formal, slightly flowery Spanish. The chief replied with equal courtesy. Only then, as Carlos drew her into the center of the group, did he turn his assessing gaze on Leigh.

A moment or two passed while she was subjected to a close, sharp scrutiny. Then the old man gave a deep sigh. He nodded. "It is as you claimed, Carlos Wainwright," he said. "Her features reflect the truth that you spoke. Therefore, I concur. It is right that she be allowed to hear the full story."

Looking much relieved, Carlos turned to Leigh. "Niza wishes to speak to you about an important matter."

Since there was a chance that the other two men were unfamiliar with English, Carlos had continued to speak in Spanish as a courtesy to them. Leigh followed his lead when it seemed obvious that she was expected to say something. Trying not to show how awed she was to be here in this strange place under these mysterious circumstances, she inclined her head to Niza, indicating her respect, and then she thanked him for welcoming her to the pueblo.

"I understand you have a story to tell me?" she continued.

While the chief did not unbend to the point of smiling, he seemed satisfied by her courteous behavior. Motioning for her to join him, he moved toward a pair of cane chairs.

"Sit with me and we will talk of this matter," he said. "Because it involves both your people and mine, I feel it is my duty to pass this tale on to you."

Leigh bent forward, giving him her rapt attention. She almost forgot that there was anyone else in the room except the two of them.

Some years past, Niza said, a group of braves had set out on an autumn hunting trip, as they always did at that season. Game in the mountains proved to be scarce. After a week, the hunters started back to their pueblo almost empty-handed. But when they reached the edge of the forest, they were glad not to be too heavily burdened, because there they found an unconscious man who needed their help. He had been set upon by robbers, grievously injured, and left to die. All his possessions had been stolen, Niza emphasized. There was nothing left to give any clue to his identity.

Leigh clamped her lips, fighting the urge to pour out a dozen questions at once.

The hunters stretched a skin between poles, Niza went on. They used this travois to bring the badly wounded man home to their pueblo. On arrival, he was placed in the care of the chief's daughter. A widow whose children were grown, her nursing skills were renowned throughout the area.

With a mounting agitation, Leigh contin- ued to listen. So that was the explanation! All those years she had wronged him, mistakenly assuming that he had abandoned her.

Seeing her stunned expression, Niza hurried to conclude his narration. Days later, he said, the man finally recovered consciousness. But he was able to tell his rescuers nothing about his history or what had happened to him. The blow to his head had deprived him of his memory.

For a long time he hovered between life and death. Finally, he began to recover. By the time he was well enough to walk, he and his nurse had grown extremely fond of each other. When the circuit-riding priest made his next visit to the pueblo, the couple requested that he join them in matrimony.

Leigh had no doubt now as to what the chief's reference to "your people" and "my people" had meant. "So this stranger became your son-in-law," she whispered. "What — what name does he have?"

Niza eyed her impassively. "Since it was clear from the beginning that he was a man of the soil, we called him Tiller."

How appropriate, Leigh thought. Eager for more information, she asked another question: "After Tiller's recovery, did he and your daughter leave the pueblo? Or does he still —"

But there was no need to finish the query.

Niza's eyes had strayed to the doorway. Leigh broke off, following his gaze. Framed in the opening, a man she had never expected to see again was spotlighted in the flood of noontime sunlight. Though she knew he was in his late sixties, he looked vigorous and fit.

As if in a trance, she rose from the chair and walked slowly to the door.

The man called Tiller had paused to display a massive pumpkin to two braves who had stopped to greet him on the path. He pointed to the curving green stem and the healthy orange skin of the vegetable. The younger men nodded. She could see respect on their faces as they listened to what he had to say. In turn, Tiller seemed to be congratulating them. This was how pumpkins ought to look, he seemed to be saying. All of them had done a wonderful job.

Had there been any doubt of his identity, the sound of his laughter would have instantly erased it. How well she remembered that sound. And how seldom had she heard it during the years she was growing up. Apparently, her father had far more cause for happiness these days. No one could fail to notice the natural authority with which he spoke, or the straight way he held his head and shoulders, as though he were proud to be walking the earth and contributing his share to the pueblo's prosperity. How different from the slouching posture she remembered, the hangdog look he had worn following one of DeeDee's tongue-lashings about their lack of worldly goods!

Just then a fourth person joined the group. Leigh had glimpsed the woman earlier, shoveling loaves of bread into the beehive oven. It was obvious from the actions of all three men that they considered her someone special. What a sweet face she had, Leigh thought, and what radiance there was in her smile as she beamed up at Tiller. But his expression spoke even more loudly. He was regarding that plump, middle-aged woman with the kind of reverential love that a glamorous movie star would trade her Oscar to win from a man!

With a parting comment, the younger men walked away. Tiller turned. In that moment he became aware of the young woman standing in the doorway of the communal room.

Leigh's lips parted to call out a glad greeting. But before she could speak or take the first step to run forward and throw her arms around Hoyt Sinclair, Carlos's hand stole into hers and gave a squeeze.

"He never regained his memory, *querida*," he whispered.

With a startled gasp, she drew back. The final truth dawned on her. She still didn't have a father, Leigh realized. Not one who knew her. And unless she insisted on dragging Tiller away from a life where he had finally found happiness and achieved self-respect, she never would have.

For all practical purposes, the person the world had known as Hoyt Sinclair really did die out there in the wilderness. From his blank stare, she knew that Tiller had no recollection of either his old life or the daughter he had left behind.

It isn't fair! she wanted to howl. Finding him but not being able to claim him as the father she had always adored was a cruel twist of fate. But she was no longer a child. Leigh forced herself to view the situation from a grown-up attitude. Now, at last, her father had found the contentment and serenity and love that had for so many years eluded him. And even more, he had found self-esteem, and earned respect from the people among whom he lived. He had the satisfaction of contributing, of sharing his skills with others.

She couldn't destroy all that for him. At the very least, massive confusion was bound to result if she tried to reacquaint him with the past. Niza and his kindhearted daughter, as well as Tiller, would have their lives disrupted. She realized now why the chief had been so reluctant to share his tale with her. If his son-in-law learned about his former life, a decision would be forced upon him: stay, or return to Santa Fe? If he returned, what kind of life would he find in town? Without a doubt, his departure would disrupt the whole village.

Leigh was not willing to step in and destroy the happiness of others to gratify a selfish purpose of her own. Turning aside from Tiller's impersonal gaze as though they were strangers whose eyes had happened to meet, she moved back inside the room.

"Thank you, Carlos, for bringing me here," she said softly. "Proving that my father never intended to abandon me was the most wonderful gift you could ever give me. How did you find out what had happened to him?"

"From the very beginning, I was convinced that your father wouldn't have walked away from you permanently. Not on purpose. It would have been completely out of character for the type of man you had described to me. But at the time of your dad's disappearance, you had filed a missing-persons report and asked the authorities to investigate. I didn't see what I could do at this late date. It wasn't until the nuns came to Santa Fe for the language courses that I got to thinking about all the remote places they visit. There are always little schools on the reservations. And people will talk to a new teacher. . . ."

Suddenly, Leigh remembered a visit he had made to his aunt shortly after his return from Oklahoma City. He must have asked Mother Superior to help him spread the word about the missing man through all the different religious orders in the state. No wonder he hadn't wanted her to come along that day. The odds were heavily against anything ever coming of his idea. He didn't want to get her hopes up, then see her disappointed again.

"Incredible as it seems, the idea worked," Carlos went on. "A nun I had never even met sent word back to Santa Fe that an Anglo man had been living in this pueblo for several years. Tia Carmelita arranged by mail for me to come and meet Sister Agnes. Because she was here teaching the children and had learned to communicate in Keresan, she was able to introduce me to Niza. He didn't really want to talk to me — in any language. But I guess his sympathy was aroused when I told him about the wonderful girl I intended to marry, and about her father who had disappeared years ago."

"Oh, Carlos, thank you so much for persisting! And how good of all the sisters to take the time to help." Leigh blinked back tears. "You only meant for me to learn what had happened to him, didn't you? And not disrupt his life by trying to drag him back to Santa Fe."

Approval of her decision glowed in his eyes. "One of the reasons I love you, darling, is that you always think of others before yourself. Me, Kit, Gail — even Roger. I knew you wouldn't do anything to distress another human being. But I was also anxious to have you find this out before our wedding. Now, even though it will still be Kit who gives you away, you'll have the confidence of knowing your own father did love you. And that he didn't deliberately go off and abandon you."

That knowledge would make a tremendous difference to her outlook and morale, Leigh realized. Never again would she worry about Carlos turning his back on her, as she'd always believed that her parents had done. And when she met his parents for the first time, she could hold her head high. After all, she'd had a father who loved her as much as they loved their son.

"I'm so glad Niza's people found him,"

she said tremulously. "They did more than save his life. They offered their love and friendship, and restored to him a sense of self-worth that living with DeeDee and losing his ranch had stolen from him. I would never dream of jeopardizing that."

She glanced outside. The path was empty. Tiller and his wife had strolled on to resume their daily lives. It was time for her and Carlos to do the same.

Leigh returned to the spot where Niza sat. "I owe you more than I can say," she told him. "For sharing that story with me, and for all your kindness to Tiller. Anyone can see he is very happy here. Thank you again, for everything."

Then she took the hand of her future husband and walked with him out into the sunlight. She knew that she would never look back again. The past was history.

And the future was theirs to share.